A collection of stories centered around Christmas cookies.

Spellbooks and Shortbread by Denise D. Young

Secret Family Recipes for Love and Butter Cookies by Melissa McTernan

Chocolate Chip Christmas Wishes by Nicole McCaffrey

A Scoop of Pecans

by

Denise D. Young
Melissa McTernan
Nicole McCaffrey

A Scoop of Pecans

The Wild Rose Press, Inc.
PO Box 708
Adams Basin, NY 14410-0708
Visit us at www.thewildrosepress.com

Publishing History
First Edition, 2022
Trade Paperback ISBN 978-1-5092-4483-6

Published in the United States of America

Spellbooks and Shortbread

by

Denise D. Young

Christmas Cookies Series

Chapter One

I wrinkled my nose at the stench of garbage. *Yuck.* That scent didn't exactly fill me with the Christmas spirit.

Well, Juniper, that's what you get for teleporting into an alley behind a diner.

The alley—in Mount Holly, Pennsylvania, site of my next heist—was filled with gray, slushy snow. A giant, green dumpster shielded me from prying eyes should some passerby happen to glance in my direction.

The crackle of green magic that had transported me to this place dissipated as I rubbed the amulet at my throat.

Hopefully the rest of Mount Holly didn't smell this bad.

Best get this over with. I wasn't here for the eggnog, after all.

As a thief for hire by trade and a faerie by birth, I had one reason for being in Mount Holly—thievery, plain and simple.

Normally, I'd be miles away from human civilization on Christmas Eve, hiding in some remote corner of the Faerie Realm and ignoring basically everyone.

But this job was easy money, and I *was* a thief, after all. I wasn't going to say no to a job that paid well and had minimal risk of losing life and limb.

A member of the Order of Magicks, a secret society of the world's most elite and powerful mages and wizards, had summoned me just hours earlier. Apparently, a careless wizard had let a spellbook full of rather powerful spells fall into human hands—an unsuspecting bookstore owner in a small Pennsylvania town.

"We don't need another dark age, need I remind you," Oliver Nichols had said grimly as he peered at me from behind a gargantuan mahogany desk, surrounded by leather-clad magical tomes and crystalline orbs.

Oliver had a long, white beard, twinkling blue eyes, a penchant for pocket watches, and an annoying tendency to laugh at his own jokes. I kind of liked him anyway.

I spun a globe that rested on a carved wooden stand, the polished surface squeaking beneath my fingernail as the sphere turned. "Does he know what he has?"

"Not a clue." His lips quirked upward as he spoke, as though the mark's obliviousness were a source of small delight. "But speed is of the essence. If some unaffiliated mage gets ahold of it, I shudder to think what could happen. The stakes might be high, but the job itself should be quick and painless. And don't worry about the owner, Magnus. He won't suspect a thing."

"Why me?" I was at the height of my profession, and my prices weren't cheap. Surely some rogue faerie thief would do such a job for far less.

"You're going to be among humans. Discretion is key."

"Of course." No need to out the magical community to a town full of mortals, right? The cleanup would be far too much hassle and expense. Memory spells alone cost a pretty penny—not to mention the fines the order would face from the Council of Magical Beings.

With that, I'd changed into standard human attire, packed a bag, and followed the spell Oliver had given me into Mount Holly.

I tugged on a pair of black, tight-fitting, calfskin gloves. I'd chosen a purple plaid jacket and a black beanie, a pair of black jeans, and a black turtleneck underneath. I could lose the colorful jacket when needed, but a woman walking around in all black in a small town on Christmas Eve *might* draw some suspicion.

I stepped out of the alley, zipping my jacket up farther against the cold. A light snow had just begun to fall.

"Goblin's bones," I cursed as I rounded the corner onto Main Street, catching my first glimpse of Mount Holly.

I'd expected the bustling streets, the streetlamps with their Christmas lights and evergreen wreaths, the package-laden passersby, the occasional notes of a Christmas tune drifting toward me from a nearby store.

What I hadn't expected was the giant sign draped across Main Street. *Welcome to Mount Holly. The Christmas Capital of Pennsylvania!* And another that proclaimed *37th Annual Holly Festival, Christmas Eve.*

The street had been closed to vehicles, and it was crammed with people. Carolers stood on one street corner, huddled together as they prepared to burst into a rendition of some beloved holiday tune. Vendors were lined up, selling everything from mittens to quilts to homemade jerky to hot chocolate. And festivalgoers milled, elbow to elbow, making the space far too claustrophobic for my taste.

Hell.

I was in hell.

No wonder Oliver had seemed so amused when I left his office. He knew. Send the misanthropic loner faerie to rob a bookstore on Christmas Eve in a town that walked, talked, and breathed Christmas spirit?

Oh, if I had the nerve to curse a wizard as powerful as Oliver, I totally would.

The girl at the hot-chocolate stand, a teenager with bleached hair that had been dyed pale pink, waved at me. "Would you like a cocoa? It's three dollars. Proceeds benefit the local animal shelter."

Ugh. I wanted to tell her flat-out no, but the juxtaposition of her black fingernail polish and her ugly Christmas sweater featuring a kitten with a ball of yarn about did me in.

"Sure." I sighed and fished a few crisp dollar bills out of my pocket and handed them to her.

She filled a paper to-go cup with steamy cocoa. "I love your hair."

"Uh, thanks," I muttered. I was actually relieved that colorful hair dye was in style now; it meant I no longer had to use a glamour spell to hide my hair's naturally occurring green streaks.

A quick glance around the packed street told me I would have to wait until this crowd thinned out before I could get the job done. And the festivalgoers seemed both undaunted by the cold *and* buoyed by Christmas joy. Which meant it would be a while.

"What brand did you use to dye it?" the girl continued.

"Oh, it's natural." I glanced around, still distracted.

Crap. The look she gave me said she thought I was

one hundred percent weird.

I smiled. "I'm kidding."

"Oh." She gave a small laugh.

A minute later, having extracted myself from hearing about the new cat wing at the local animal shelter, I was caught in the sea of the crowd, sipping hot cocoa with peppermint syrup and whipped cream because, well, why not? It was all on the order's dime, after all. The carolers burst into an exuberant rendition of "Walking in a Winter Wonderland" while snowflakes whirled in the sky.

It was all merriment and bustle and joy.

In short, pure torture.

I wrinkled my nose, temples pulsing with a growing headache. Sensory overload—too many people, too many sounds. The joyful singing of the carolers combined with chatter, laughter, even the clanging of a metal lid from the stand of a nearby vendor selling soup.

I tossed the empty paper cup into a nearby trash can and searched for a way out. A cacophony of scents, sounds, and images blended and blurred together. A tension headache formed a tight band around my skull.

I bet Oliver and his husband, Walter, were sipping mulled wine with their fellow wizards and laughing their asses off about this.

I glanced past the crowd, desperate for a reprieve.

There.

I spotted it in the chaos, a small bit of sanctuary.

The Village Bookshop, the sign read, gilded script a flourish against classic hunter green. Despite the display of Christmas books in the window—everything from *The Polar Express* to a holiday-themed romance complete with a beagle and mitten-clad couple on the cover—the bookstore offered me two things.

One, a bit of peace and quiet.

Two, a chance to case the place.

I tugged my gloves up farther and sidestepped a little girl in an impossibly frilly red dress who was dancing on the sidewalk to the carolers' "Frosty the Snowman" while the crowd cooed in delight.

No, my lips did *not* just quirk up in a smile, I assured myself.

A bell jangled as I opened the door.

It closed behind me, muffling the sounds of the festivalgoers.

Ahhh. Sweet relief.

The Village Bookshop wasn't exactly the sort of place one would expect to find a dangerous book of magic.

It was, well, quite ordinary. Worn but comfy-looking couches and chairs offered cozy spots for reading while handmade wooden signs pointed customers in the direction of various genres. Tabletop displays featured local authors, winter- and holiday-themed reads, and cookbooks.

"Looking for anything in particular or just browsing?" a male voice full of Scottish brogue asked.

I glanced up to see six feet two of man towering over me. My mouth was suddenly parched. Brown, slightly unruly hair framed a face with a strong jaw and brown eyes under long eyelashes. His complexion was ruddy and his frame muscled—not the bent-backed elderly man I'd expected at all when Oliver had described Magnus MacDougal, owner of The Village Bookshop.

Toss in the Scottish accent, and he was killing me softly. Definitely the complete package.

I swallowed and forced a smile. "Just browsing," I managed to say.

He offered me a smile in return. My stomach did a flip-flop.

No. None of that. I'm not here for hanky-panky. Certainly not with the mark.

"Let me know if I can help you find anything," he said, that accent sliding over me once more. "We're closing soon, though."

I nodded and disappeared into the store. New books were displayed at the ends of the rows while the long, wooden shelves beyond contained a surprisingly excellent selection of gently used books.

I was flipping through the occult and new-age section, hoping I might get lucky but beginning to doubt it, when the bell jangled again.

"Dad! We raised three hundred and seventy-two dollars for the shelter!" a teenage voice yelled.

"Shh. We have a customer, Kenzie," the bookstore owner with the delightful brogue said.

I glanced up in time to see him ruffle his daughter's hair as she tried to sidestep him. It was the girl from the cocoa stand.

"Sorry." She lowered her voice. "Think how happy the cats will be, though." She then plopped down in one of the overstuffed chairs, resting her feet on a coffee table and scrolling through her phone.

Magnus stepped into the back, and I caught a glimpse of an office that contained, among other things, a small safe. I didn't see any security cameras, and a quick search with my magic told me there weren't any. The safe looked pretty standard—I'd make easy work of it with my faerie magic. That *had* to be where the book was.

Just to be sure the book wasn't mixed into the inventory, I spent a few more minutes flipping through the shelves and coming up with nada.

This didn't seem like the sort of place one would find a dangerous spellbook.

I almost wondered if Oliver had sent me on a wild goose chase.

Except the amount of coin he'd already transferred into my bank vault back in the Faerie Realm suggested he was dead serious.

I gave up and, sneaking a peek over my shoulder at Magnus and Kenzie, crept toward my favorite section.

The walls were painted with flowers and fairies, a pastoral scene with livestock surrounding a cottage where poppies grew and pixies flew on glittering wings. The table and chairs were impossibly small, even for a little four-feet-eleven woman like myself. But I didn't care.

My fingers tingled with anticipation as they grazed the spines of books. I seized a copy of the book I wanted. My all-time favorite, Hans Christian Andersen's *The Snow Queen*. This one had gorgeous watercolor illustrations as it told the story of Gerda and Kai. I let myself get lost in the familiar tale, following Gerda on her journey to rescue her beloved friend, the rich illustrations drawing me further into the tale.

The gentle clearing of a throat interrupted my journey.

I shook my head, coming out of a trance. Some thief I was. Instead of casing the place, I was curled up in the corner, feet tucked underneath me, the mural framing me while I read. I'd even taken my boots off at some point.

Magnus knelt beside me, the look on his face one of amusement. "Far be it for me to disturb your adventures." His voice, rich and deep like dark chocolate, left little tingles of heat in its wake. "But it's closing time. I promised my daughter I'd take her to the cookie contest."

The heat of a blush crept into my cheeks. I'd basically gone and made myself a nest in his bookstore. "Of course. I'm sorry."

"Never apologize for getting lost in a good book. Especially not that one. It's one of my favorites. Not nearly as sad as some of Hans Christian Andersen's other works."

"I know. When I was a kid, I read *The Little Matchstick Girl* and cried for days," I blurted out. My cheeks grew hotter. Why would I go and say a thing like that? I'd never told anyone that story. Never.

He nodded. "That one was heartbreaking. I prefer the ones with happy endings."

I tried to picture this tall, handsome man, with his serious, thoughtful eyes, reading one of the romance novels I'd seen on display. Nope. Couldn't see it.

"I wouldn't take you for the fairy-tale type," I admitted. "I figured you for more of a Thomas Hardy man."

"Hardy?" He waggled his eyebrows. "Oh, I hardly read Hardy these days."

I couldn't help but laugh at the pun.

He offered me a hand to help me up, and I accepted, though it was far from necessary. His palm engulfed my smaller hand, his skin warm against mine. The scent of woodsy cologne and supple leather wafted toward me.

More tingles.

No. I couldn't afford the luxury of attraction.

"You're the first person to ever laugh at that joke," he said. "I try to read as widely as possible. But fairy tales are my favorite. And folk tales. My mother and uncle love telling and retelling those sorts of stories. I guess they stuck with me. My uncle especially can spin a fantastical tale so well he could make you believe it."

I caught a glimpse of Magnus's aura as he spoke, sky blue with deeper crackles of cobalt. Blue auras meant wisdom, kindness, and a gift for communication. He would be eloquent and kind, I imagined, the sort of man who'd tend to a wounded bird just as easily as he would give a rousing, impassioned speech to save a historic building from demolition.

The book I'd been holding slipped from my hand, tumbling to the hardwood floor.

My blush was no doubt straight-up crimson now.

"I'm so sorry," I mumbled.

He chuckled and swept the book off the floor. "No worries. I've dropped a few books in my day. They usually survive."

He closed the book and slid it back into its spot on the shelf, the motion smooth and studied, no doubt from years of habit.

"I'll let you close up." I shrugged on my jacket and quickly tied my boots.

He studied me, his gaze lingering. I shouldn't have spent time talking to him, letting him see my face—let alone have the guy check me out.

"It was nice to meet you, Miss…"

"Juniper. Juniper Whitethorn."

"Juniper," he repeated.

Crap. If I had to give my name, I would give my

nickname—June. It was more forgettable and more common—both good things for a thief. And even then I would give my first name only.

Blame it on Christmas or the festival or Magnus's gaze, but I'd slipped up.

"I'm Magnus."

To my credit, I did manage not to tell him I already knew his name—Oliver had told me that much. What he hadn't told me was the guy was like a cup of tea with honey—both hot and sweet. But then, Oliver had left out quite a few important details.

As the door closed behind me, my faerie hearing picked up Kenzie's words. "We're going to be late," she groused.

"We have plenty of time," he assured her.

Typical father-daughter banter.

Then, as he flipped the sign from open to closed, she added, "Were you flirting with her?"

Now *his* face was that flustered shade of crimson.

I dove into the crowd before my uncanny fae ears could catch any more of their conversation.

Truthfully, I didn't want to know. I had a job to do.

And Christmas Eve flirtations were *not* in my job description.

Chapter Two

The vendors were packing up their stands, a few snowflakes drifting toward the ground. I sidestepped a woman pulling a wagon full of embroidered tea towels and pot holders, then backpedaled quickly as an elderly man carrying a large gift basket featuring various smoked meats and hot sauces nearly plowed into me.

Ugh. Crowds.

At least the carolers were gone, and all I was left with was the din of vendors discussing their holiday plans and the local gossip—apparently, the town had let a local golden retriever take part in a live nativity scene with comedic and chaotic results.

"So I guess Milo wasn't such a good boy, after all," I muttered under my breath, laughing at my own joke.

That was the sort of holiday shenanigan I could get behind.

"Hello!" a bracingly loud voice bellowed from behind me. I spun around, a bit like a sheep hearing the wolf's howl.

A tall, slender woman with a stylish blond coif, her frame clad in a crimson peacoat trimmed with white fur, was waving at me.

Furiously waving.

I sighed but plastered on a smile. "Hi?"

"I just realized you might be one of our festival tourists, and I wanted to make sure you were enjoying our Annual Holly Festival."

"It's great." I tucked my hands into my pockets.

"I'm Mayor Greenwood, and I just wanted to say welcome."

Before I could stop her, she was seizing my hand and shaking it vigorously. My magic crackled, threatening to come to life, but I tamped it down.

I eyed the crowd, looking for an escape route. "Thanks. I, uh, have to get going."

"Oh, are you coming to the cookie contest?" she asked with so much extroverted energy and enthusiasm it made my head hurt.

"I, uh…was actually heading out."

Okay, truth be told, I was going to case the bookstore from a nearby alley until I was sure Magnus and his daughter were long gone, then grab the spellbook and run. But mum *was* the operative word.

"Oh, not before you come to the cookie contest, dear." She looped her arm into mine, called out a hello to another passerby, and whisked me away.

My whole life, I'd been a thief.

And now I was being stolen away—against my will, hauled to a Christmas cookie contest.

"Where are you from, my dear? I'm so sorry—what was your name?"

"June."

"June. Lovely name. I had an aunt named June. Well, great-aunt, on my mother's side. Now, her almond cookies won the cookie contest twice. I've tried, but I could never get mine to come out quite right. But my macaroons could give that Magnus MacDougal a run for his money."

That was right—Magnus MacDougal would be at

this thing. And he'd already seen my face enough times. The last thing I needed was to be the mayor's guest of honor at a local bakeoff.

"Is that so?" I tried to keep my tone casual, even if the idea of the handsome bookstore owner donning an apron and baking cookies did tickle my fancy—just a little.

"Oh yes. Have you met him?" Her tone wasn't at all casual. It oozed curiosity, as if she were just itching for a bit of juicy small-town gossip.

"I briefly visited the bookstore earlier today."

"Oh, lovely. If you go back, be sure to pick up a copy of *The Pontist's Photographic Guide to the Bridges of Lancaster County*. My cousin wrote it. It's all about our fine region's beautiful covered bridges. He took the photographs himself. 'Pontist' means someone who's a historic bridge enthusiast. Neil—my cousin—explained that in his talk at the library in September."

No. The spell hadn't worked. Maybe I wasn't in Mount Holly after all. I'd bonked my head, and I was lying unconscious somewhere—maybe in a warm bed back in the Faerie Realm or at the Order of Magicks's headquarters, with Oliver and his fellow wizards clucking and fussing over me.

That had to be it.

"Did you say Magnus bakes?" I was desperate to stop her from telling me the best bridges to visit during my stay. Short of running away from Mayor Greenwood, a subject change seemed the best solution.

"Mmhmm. Best shortbread in Mount Holly. Something of a legend. But he hasn't made it in six years, not since Alice left."

"Alice?"

"His wife. Well, ex-wife. Thankfully. I never liked her. Always looked down her nose at everyone in Mount Holly. He could do so much better. But after she left him and that sweet little girl of theirs for that actor, he stopped entering the contest. Too busy, he says. But you know what I think?"

No. But I had a feeling I was about to.

"Heartbreak. She broke the poor man's heart."

"And his spatula along with it?" I quipped.

Mayor Greenwood giggled. "You're too much, June."

Finally, we reached our apparent destination and stepped into the crowded community room of the Mount Holly Public Library.

If her chatter about bridges hadn't been enough to drive me over the edge, surely the press of bodies, the bright fluorescent lights, and the cacophony of voices would.

Part of me longed for quiet and solitude. I hadn't had a good Christmas in a very long time. My mother had died young, and my stepfather had helped me hone my faerie magic to learn how to become the best thief possible. Until I met Oliver and the order, no one had shown me how to use my magic for something that served anything close to the greater good. At least when Oliver called on me, it was to steal something dangerous from someone who intended to use said artifact for nefarious purposes or to save someone unknowing and innocent before that artifact could harm them.

But as far as my stepfather had been concerned, Christmas was the most wonderful time of the year to find an easy mark. I'd never had a Christmas gift that wasn't stolen—not since I was ten and my mother had passed.

"Mayor Greenwood!" a familiar voice called. Kenzie came running up, cheeks flushed, hair mussed. "I don't think we have enough cups for the refreshments table."

The mayor turned to me and patted my arm. "Please excuse me. Enjoy the contest. It does get quite heated." With a small wave, she began weaving her way through the crowd.

Kenzie leaned forward. "Are you okay? I got here as quickly as I could."

I nodded. "I may yet survive." I placed the back of my hand against my forehead and pretended to swoon. "You did cut it awfully close, you know." But I couldn't help following that up with a conspiratorial wink. The little trickster had just concocted a cup shortage to save me, after all.

She grinned at me. "Well, it took me a while to hide the cups."

I laughed out loud—a real laugh, deep from my belly. "You little thief," I said playfully.

She just shrugged. "Don't tell my dad." She began to step away but turned back. "You can sign up at that table over there, by the way. To be a judge."

"I don't want to be a judge," I grumbled.

"Don't worry. You just eat a bunch of cookies and fill out a scoresheet. It's completely anonymous. That's the fun thing about our contest. Everyone's a judge. Dad says it's democracy in action. I call it *The Great British Bakeoff* meets *American Idol*."

I caught a whiff of cookies—chocolate chip, cinnamon, scents spicy and sweet all blending together to tempt me.

"I do enjoy *The Great British Bakeoff*," I admitted. That wasn't a lie.

I should've gone back to the bookstore. I should've grabbed the book and run. But she stood there expectantly, and I sighed.

"I'm Kenzie, by the way." She walked me to the signup table.

"I'm June." *There*. How hard was that? Nickname given. Unlike my slipup with Magnus.

Another girl about Kenzie's age came up to us, and the two grabbed their scoresheets and ran off, leaving me alone. Across the room, I spied Magnus, head bent as he listened intently to an older gentleman, nodding occasionally.

As if sensing my gaze, he glanced up. Our eyes locked, and heat sizzled in me again.

I should've walked away. The bookstore was empty. I could grab the book and run.

Magnus's brief look left my heart racing.

No. Get in. Get the job done. Get paid. I knew the drill.

But I didn't follow the steps that had grown to be simple habit.

Instead, I took my "judge's badge"—a paper name tag with a holly sticker and my name written on it in permanent marker—and a scoresheet and prepared to eat my weight in cookies.

****

Fifteen minutes later, I was trying to figure out how to rate an oatmeal raisin cookie on a scale of one to five in terms of flavor, smell, texture, presentation, and creativity. Flavor? Two out of five—way too much cinnamon. Texture, three—a tad dry and crumbly.

Presentation and creativity? I gave a four in each category, because, I mean, it was oatmeal raisin, and how creative could someone be?

"Be nice," a warm, masculine voice said over my shoulder.

Something in me nearly melted as Magnus MacDougal stepped up to me, handing me a cup of water to wash down the cookie.

He peered at my scoresheet, crow's feet crinkling at the corners of his eyes. "Four for creativity? That's generous since everybody in town knows Elvira Peabody has been entering that same recipe every year since the contest started."

"No peeking." I made a show of hiding my scoresheet.

He shrugged and shot me a devilish smile. "I couldn't help it. I was curious. I didn't think I'd see you here. Didn't figure you for the cookie-contest type."

"It's cookies." I grinned at him and reached for the next entry—some sort of cookie with a spoonful of jam in the center. "Not exactly controversial. Or did you think I wasn't any fun?"

He took a sip from his paper cup. "You didn't seem like the sort who liked crowds. I figured that was why you were hiding out in my bookshop."

"Oh…that." I swallowed a piece of cookie and gave it a four for flavor. Good, but whoever baked those gingersnaps I'd tasted earlier would be hard to beat. "That story is just one of my favorites."

"Mine too." He reached for another cookie— number fourteen, one with pecans in it and a buttery scent. "The way Gerda would do anything to rescue Kai."

I nodded. An old sadness stirred in me. Because, if I was honest, maybe I wanted someone to care about me that much—even if I had learned a long time ago to rescue myself.

"I'm sorry. I've said something." His face was instant concern, his brows knitting together, wrinkles creasing his forehead.

I shook my head. "No. Not really a fan of, you know, all the deck-the-halls hubbub is all."

"So you came to a Christmas festival to escape all the yuletide merriment?"

We each circled numbers on our scoresheets as we talked, finishing tasting the last couple of cookies on the table.

I laughed. "Yeah. I'm a genius."

He chuckled, the sound warm, inviting. Why did this man I'd just met, with those deep brown eyes that contrasted with his navy-blue pullover, feel like a toasty fire on a chilly night?

"You have…" He brushed his thumb against my jaw. "Sorry. Bit of jam."

Our eyes locked. For a split second, the crowd and its chatter fell away. I felt…safe. His scent wrapped around me, like leather and woodsmoke.

A smile tugged at my lips. "Thanks."

The screech of sound-system feedback shattered the spell. I winced as Mayor Greenwood tapped on a microphone, yoo-hooing as she did so.

"Let's hand in our scoresheets, everyone! We'll get everyone's votes tallied and—"

Before she could finish, a clap of thunder sounded overhead.

Actual thunder. In December.

The lights went out, and the entire room plunged into pure darkness.

Gasps and chatter filled the room.

"Stay calm, everyone! Probably a transformer blew," Mayor Greenwood bellowed over the crowd.

Pinpricks of bright lights flickered to life as people grabbed their phones and flipped on their flashlight apps. My fae eyesight adapted to the darkness easily, though—it was one of the things that made me a top-notch thief.

I winced at the onslaught of light and stumbled, reaching for the closest thing to hold on to.

What I found were Magnus's arms. Those muscled arms wrapped around me, tugging me against him—not tight enough to feel trapped, but firmly enough to feel safe.

"Are you all right, Juniper?" His soothing murmur caressed each syllable of my full name.

"Yes," I whispered, the single word throaty.

How did he do that?

My whole life, crowds, too many sights, too many sounds, overwhelmed me, sent me running, my head spinning.

In his arms, despite the chaos of the crowd, the din of surprised chatter, the strobe-like nature of flashlight beams from smartphones, I felt calm.

Had I ever felt calm? Not since my mother's passing. Even when I was alone, I was still running.

Magnus's hands moved in comforting circles against my back. I leaned farther into him, tilting my face toward his. I pressed my hands against his chest, his heart thundering beneath his sweater.

We were in the shadows now, tucked into a little corner away from the chaos. I could feel the flicker of desire in his energy field, and I definitely felt my own desire building.

Would anyone see us, in the dark, if we kissed, like two teenagers under the bleachers? What would it be like to have a moment of calm in a world that, day after day, was chaos and noise?

I looked up at him. His gaze sought my face in the dark, though I knew he couldn't see me nearly as well as my fae eyes saw him. His right hand fell away from my back, his fingers sliding up my arm, brushing my hair from my cheek to tilt my face farther toward his.

"Dad?" Kenzie's voice broke the spell of desire.

Magnus released me so hard I stumbled, bracing myself against a nearby table.

"Kenzie. Are you okay?" He sounded as if he were coming out of a trance.

Yeah. We both needed to come back to reality a little, didn't we?

Fortunately, no one could see what I was sure was a vibrant crimson flush in my cheeks as desire gave way to embarrassment.

Nothing could happen between me and Magnus—not even a stolen kiss in a shadowy corner.

Thieves did *not* get happy endings or magical Christmases. I needed to remember that.

"I'm fine." If Kenzie sensed anything had been happening, she didn't mention it. "Sophie's dad said the power is out all over town."

"I guess we'd better head home, then," he said.

I tried to ignore the knot that formed in my stomach at those words. Oliver had mentioned they lived in an apartment above the bookstore, but I wasn't worried. With my magic, I could slip in and out of the bookstore undetected. I just had to wait for them to fall asleep.

And then I could do what I came to Mount Holly to do—pull a reverse Santa Claus.

In the light of her cell phone, concern filled Kenzie's big, bright eyes. "What about the storm?"

"What storm?" Magnus said.

"The freak snowstorm that just started. Everyone's talking about it." She pulled up a video on her phone, a clip on a social media site of a girl a couple of years her senior filming herself in front of a window that showed blizzard-like conditions beyond.

"Everyone stay calm! We're concluding the festivities early tonight," Mayor Greenwood yelled, her voice an octave higher than it had been before. It was the least calming way to tell people to stay calm I'd ever heard. "Please head toward your vehicles in an orderly fashion. Drive safely, and Merry Christmas!"

People began moving toward the exit in a not-so-orderly fashion.

Magnus tugged my arm and Kenzie's and drew us back into a nook out of the way. "Best wait for the crowd to thin out a bit."

"Dad, I want to get home soon." In the dark, Kenzie snuggled into her dad's side, the feisty teenager façade fading away for a moment. "Luna is probably lonely. What if she's scared?"

"Oh, I doubt that. Cats aren't afraid of the dark." He wrapped an arm around his daughter.

My heart went out to her. She was just a scared kid who wanted her dad and her cat on Christmas Eve.

"It's true," I assured her, squeezing her shoulder. "In fact, cats prefer the dark. She's probably having the time of her life playing with her favorite toy."

She nodded.

"Why don't you stay here with June?" he said to her, shooting me a glance.

I nodded, trying not to consider the irony of keeping watch over the daughter of the man I was sent to rob.

And trying to ignore the knot in my stomach that tightened with guilt.

"I'll go get the car warmed up, then." Magnus patted his daughter on the back before heading out the double doors of the library, tucking his hands into his pockets and ducking his head against the snow.

Kenzie and I settled into our little nook while the rest of the throng vanished.

"Do you have any fun videos on there?" I jutted my chin toward her phone. I didn't have one of the infernal devices personally but found them sort of fascinating.

"Anything you want. Want to see people falling down in the snow? There's a video channel that's nothing but that."

"Always."

We giggled over ski fails, snow fails, and even one guy trying to ride a unicycle in the snow.

A few minutes later, her phone buzzed.

"It's my dad. He's waiting out front with the car. He says the roads are probably bad." She glanced at me. "Did you drive here?"

"I walked," I told her. "I don't drive."

She frowned, her brow a furrow of teenage concern. "How will you get back to your house?"

"Oh, I don't live in Mount Holly. Just visiting. But I walk everywhere. Don't worry."

Her eyebrows rose. "Even in a blizzard? You're weird, June. Really weird."

I quirked one of my eyebrows in response. "Good weird or bad weird?"

She cocked her head. "I haven't decided yet." She stood and slipped her jacket on. Before she walked away, she turned to me and gave me a wave in the dark. "Merry Christmas."

"Merry Christmas." I waved back.

She vanished through the door to the community room. I stood. Better leave as well before I got wrangled into cleanup duty. I slid my judge's sheet into the waiting box on my way out the door.

Pity. I kind of wanted to stick around and see who won.

More than that, I kind of wanted to stick around and taste Magnus MacDougal's shortbread.

No. That moment in his arms, my hands splayed across his chest, came back to me, a surge of warmth with it.

I wanted far more than a taste of Magnus MacDougal.

And that really was a pity—because now I had to go wait for him to fall asleep so I could rob him.

Chapter Three

I stepped out the double doors of the Mount Holly Public Library—a one-story building clad in gray stone with rounded windows, like something out of an old English village.

I didn't normally care for human towns and cities. But Mount Holly had a quality about it even I found appealing—a coziness, an inviting warmth that drew me in.

I wrapped my jacket tighter as I walked through the swiftly falling snow. If it kept this up, we'd have a foot on the ground by morning—easily.

But I'd be long gone by then, I reminded myself. With my little side adventure at the cookie contest behind me, I needed to refocus.

The streets were mostly deserted now, people heading home to their families. The storm had started out of nowhere, but already a snow truck went by, ensuring at least Main Street in town was momentarily clear.

The windows of the shops and restaurants were dark. Where many small towns had downtowns full of shuttered storefronts, Mount Holly seemed to be alive and well. An antique shop, an old-timey barber shop, a coffee shop, candy store, toy store, a place that sold pet food and supplies, Magnus's bookstore, and an assortment of restaurants graced the small-town center.

I imagined that come summer, vendors would be

selling fresh-cut flowers from brightly colored carts. An image flitted through my mind, unbidden, of Magnus handing me such a bundle.

Irises, hollyhocks, and bells of Ireland. My favorites, all tied with a bit of ribbon…

Oh. No.

I could *not* have a crush on my mark. Lusting after the guy was one thing. But a schoolgirl crush?

No. Strictly forbidden.

No emotions. Hadn't I learned that early on?

Get in. Do the job. Get out. It's not about emotion. It's about getting paid.

My stepfather's words echoed in my head. He was rotting in a faerie prison somewhere far away, in another realm, long gone from my life.

But for some reason, I'd kept going.

Maybe it was all I knew—getting in, doing the job, getting out. Getting paid.

Sigh.

A gust of icy wind battered me, and I shivered.

I was cold and alone in the dark on Christmas Eve, and recalling the warmth of the cookie contest and the pleasantness of Magnus and Kenzie's company only made me feel that much colder and lonelier.

I walked down the street, past the bookstore. At some point, the electricity flickered back to life, streetlamps casting pools of golden light amid the falling snow.

The light in the apartment above was still on. No doubt Magnus would be awake for a few more hours. My magic would help me get in and out without tripping an alarm, and cracking the standard human safe wouldn't pose a problem for me.

All that was left to do then was wait.

****

A good ten inches of snow had fallen by the time the ringing of cathedral bells told me it was midnight—officially Christmas. The lights in the apartment above The Village Bookshop had flickered off fifteen minutes ago, and the apartment was dark save for the sparkle of multi-colored Christmas lights that illuminated the front window.

I stood, brushing snow off my coat, shaking my limbs out, and heading toward the door to the shop. I'd stayed out of the line of sight from the apartment—close enough that I could see movement inside but hidden from view so its occupants couldn't see me.

Butterflies danced in my stomach.

Weird. I didn't get butterflies. Not even when I'd rappelled thirty feet down into a bewitched chamber to steal a vial of poison from a mage gone bad—my last gig for the order. Not even when I'd robbed a distinguished English lord of a cursed coin and he'd set his hounds on me.

What was it about Magnus that got to me?

Oh, I knew. As I double-checked my surroundings and approached the door, I knew.

It wasn't just that he was a drop-dead gorgeous bookstore owner with an accent that could make any girl quiver. I wasn't just any girl. I was a professional thief, after all.

It was that, underneath it all, I was sure Magnus MacDougal was sweet, thoughtful, and kind. And maybe, like me, a little bit lonely.

My hand grasped the cold metal doorknob. A jolt of something shot through me just as I unlocked the door with my magic.

That jolt had nothing to do with magic.

Just guilt.

I was about to rob a single father on Christmas.

The fact that the spellbook in his possession could be harmful didn't lessen my guilt.

Magnus was a good guy. So why didn't Oliver just offer to buy the spellbook from him for a reasonable sum? Magnus would be none the wiser, and it honestly would've been cheaper than hiring me.

I drew my hand away from the door.

I'd never bothered to ask these kinds of questions before. Why now?

Green magic crackled along my hands, tiny forks of lightning, sparks like the Fourth of July, a flicker of something akin to stardust. I watched it dance along my skin.

My whole life, I'd been a fool.

Oliver and his bearded cronies were obviously playing me. Or Magnus wasn't who I thought he was.

Doubts swirled, spinning in my head until my stomach churned.

I said I didn't trust anybody, but I trusted Oliver enough to take this job. I said there were no emotions on a job, but here I was, riddled with them.

The memory of my mom's face, on our last Christmas together. She'd been sick, her face sallow and gaunt, her eyes sunken. She'd handed me a tiny box wrapped in red-and-green plaid paper and bedecked with a gold bow and matching ribbon.

My hands shook as I opened it. Inside was a silver, heart-shaped locket. The pictures inside were of the two of us—both with our green-streaked black hair and our matching green eyes.

My stepfather had sold that locket not long after she passed, just a few months later. It was just a memory now.

I blinked, tears welling in my eyes.

I turned away from the store, swiping at my cheeks, the magic long faded from my hands.

I had to get out of here, tell Oliver the job went south, make something up. I'd cut ties with the order.

Maybe I could start over, somewhere where nobody knew who—or what—I was.

Maybe one day, I could belong somewhere.

I made my way back to the alley, now filled with freshly fallen snow. Even the green dumpster looked less disgusting with its fresh coating of pure, untouched snow on its lid.

I sniffed and reached up to grasp the talisman at my neck. I closed my eyes and prepared to teleport back to the Faerie Realm, to a spot in the woods where I went whenever the world got too overwhelming or a job got too hot.

My fingers brushed the familiar filigree, my thumb sliding over the enchanted gemstone, the words of a simple transportation incantation rising on my lips…

Nothing happened.

Nothing.

I tried again.

Nada.

Again.

Zilch.

Panic rose in me. No. I couldn't be trapped here. The magic never failed me.

Another time, one more try for good measure.

But when I opened my eyes, only the darkened alley, the brick of the walls, a restaurant's side door, and the dumpster greeted me. Not some faerie woodland full of golden stags and aged trees.

I was trapped in Mount Holly. On Christmas. In a snowstorm. On a job I'd just decided would go unfinished.

I slumped against the wall, sliding down into the snow. My hands balled into tight fists, nails biting into my palms.

After a few minutes, I rose, my legs shaking.

As a faerie, I could tolerate cold weather better than a human could, but I wasn't completely impervious to frostbite and hypothermia. I didn't know if I had enough money to afford a room at the local inn down the street, if the front desk was even open after midnight on Christmas. But it was probably my best shot.

I brushed myself off as best I could and started down Main Street. I had to walk past Magnus's bookstore to get to the inn I'd seen earlier that day—the McHenry House or something along those lines.

I couldn't bring myself to look at the bookstore or up at the twinkling lights of the MacDougal family Christmas tree. I crossed the street so I wouldn't be tempted to open the door to the bookstore or glance in its darkened windows.

Head bent, I kept my gaze on the snowy sidewalk.

"Juniper?"

I glanced over. There, on the other side of the street, in the doorway of his shop, stood Magnus MacDougal.

Chapter Four

"Hi." My lips fluttered up to form a smile but failed.

Magnus was wearing pajamas—flannel with dark green stripes on black—and his hair was tousled from sleep. He squinted at me where I stood in a pool of light from a streetlamp.

"What are you doing?" The question was laced with far too much concern for my liking.

I squirmed. The silence stretched. Finally, I shrugged. "I was about to go check and see if the McHenry House has any rooms available." *Darn.* Could've phrased that better. Or I could've said *just out for a walk.* I was slipping—definitely slipping.

He frowned. "They're booked full because of the holiday. A lot of people's out-of-town family members stay there." His frown deepened. "Have you been out here all night?"

"I don't mind the cold." I backed out of the glare of the streetlight—back into the shadows where I felt safe, hidden.

Where a thief like me belonged.

"Why don't you come inside?" he said. "I'll make you some tea to get you warmed up. You must be freezing."

My heart pounded against my rib cage, my vision tunneling as he waited there in the open doorway.

I shook my head, shrinking back farther. "No.

Really. I'm fine. I actually like the cold. There's something magical about walks in the snow."

My fingers clasped the fine silver chain of my amulet as though it were some sort of lifeline.

But it wasn't.

If anything, it was a tether to the past. A past that, on this particular night, I wanted desperately to forget.

"Well, I'm wide awake—my daughter's cat really does love the dark, and the darn thing kept waking me. I would love some company and a good cup of tea." His gaze sought out mine in the shadows.

Drawn to him, I stepped forward.

"Would you join me, Juniper?"

With an entreaty like that, what else could I say?

I nodded. "Of course."

****

Magnus guided me through the bookshop and up a set of stairs in the back.

Upstairs, we stepped through another door and into his apartment.

A blast of warmth enveloped me like a hug. He clicked the door shut softly behind us, pressing a finger to his lips. "Shh…Kenzie's asleep for the night."

I smiled. Even though his daughter was a teenager, he still didn't want to wake her.

No. That wasn't it. He probably just didn't want her to see him bringing a strange woman home in the middle of the night.

"I'll take your coat," he said, his voice a soft, low murmur.

I shrugged out of it with a shiver.

"You're soaked to the bone. Let me put the kettle on and fetch you something warm and dry."

He filled a red kettle and settled it on the stove, then disappeared down a long, narrow hallway.

I untied the laces of my boots with fingers numb from the cold. A fire crackled in a gas fireplace, and the lights on the tree twinkled amid an eclectic assortment of ornaments. A gray sofa was flanked by matching armchairs, the style low and modern. Red-and-black checkered throw pillows bedecked the furniture. The carpet was a pale blue, soft beneath my sore feet. The walls were covered with family photos, some in black frames, others printed on canvas in various sizes. The air smelled like pine and something freshly baked.

Shortbread.

The kettle began to rattle, and I went into the small kitchen of the open-concept living area. I found a red canister clearly labeled *tea* and grabbed two mugs off a waiting stand. One had a small chip in it, and I rubbed my finger over it.

The home was neat and tidy but also warm and lived-in. Books were strewn about, a few cat toys dotted the floor, and one of Kenzie's sweatshirts was draped over a chair. A few dishes were piled in the sink, waiting to be washed.

Magnus emerged from a hallway that appeared to lead to the bedroom area. "Thanks for grabbing the kettle."

I nodded. "No worries." I glanced at the label on the tea bags as I poured water into the waiting mugs. "You have good taste in tea."

"Yeah, well, when you grew up across the pond, it's mandatory."

"How did you end up here?"

"I went to college in New York. I always wanted to

own a bookstore in a small town. I ended up in Mount Holly one day about a month after graduating—just passing through. I saw the storefront and knew it was meant to be."

"Sounds like a fairy tale."

"I thought so." An undertone of bitterness added some bite to the words. He shook his head, as if clearing it away. "Where are my manners? There's a bathroom just down the hall. I set a few things in there for you. I'd be happy to throw your stuff in the dryer if you'd like."

"That's not necessary." I shivered again.

He chuckled at the contradiction, and I couldn't suppress a giggle of my own.

"Okay, maybe it is," I admitted, giving him a wink as I brushed past.

"Second door on the right."

Any romantic notion that he had invited me in out of anything other than pity went right out the window when I saw my reflection.

I was a M-E-S-S. The smattering of makeup I'd applied earlier that day had run, whether from sitting out in the snow or a bit of crying, I couldn't be sure. My hair was tangled and wet.

My stomach sank. He pitied me. Of course, he did. It was as simple as that. He was a kind, generous man who saw a bedraggled woman alone on a cold, snowy Christmas Eve night.

Nothing romantic. No sparkage. This wasn't a movie. This was real life. My *real* life. And in the real life of a faerie thief, whirlwind romances didn't happen.

I washed and dried my face, then finger-combed my short hair and toweled it dry. Magnus had left me a robe folded on the seat of a small dressing table, simple and gray but plush and warm. I caught a hint of his scent mixed with the smell of lavender fabric softener as I slipped it on.

A sigh escaped my lips as I snuggled deeper into the robe. He'd even set a pair of fleece socks underneath. Purple with a smattering of black paw prints—they must've been Kenzie's.

I ignored the butterflies rising again in my gut and returned to the living area. Magnus was sitting on the sofa, his legs outstretched and resting, ankles crossed, on the walnut coffee table.

He started to stand when I walked in, but I shook my head.

"No, please. You look cozy." And he did, in his striped pajamas and wool socks. Cozy—and hot.

He tucked a bookmark into the book he'd been reading—Charles Dickens's *A Christmas Carol*.

"Are you expecting to be visited by the ghosts of past, present, and future?" I teased.

He smirked. "I don't know what to expect anymore. Not since I found you curled up in the corner of my store."

I took a mug of tea off the waiting tray on the coffee table. Next to it was a plate of shortbread and a platter of cheese, crackers, sliced salami, and a cluster of grapes. "You didn't have to do all of this for me. I don't deserve all of this." I waved my hand at the spread.

He leaned forward and frowned. "You don't deserve a cup of hot tea and a snack after spending the night on the streets in a snowstorm? You obviously don't think very highly of yourself."

I shrugged. I placed a slice of salami on top of some Havarti and a water cracker and devoured it. "It's not that. I am a woman of many talents. I know what I'm good at." Making friends wasn't one of those things. And I was even worse when it came to romance.

He studied me in the firelight, his gaze deep and curious. No one had ever looked at me like that—like I was a mystery they desperately wanted to solve. "Tell me, then, what you're good at."

Uh-oh. I'd walked right into that one. I fidgeted and helped myself to a piece of shortbread. "Wow." The buttery concoction melted in my mouth. "Mayor Greenwood wasn't kidding. Your shortbread is amazing."

He seemed pleased. But then he waggled an eyebrow. "Don't change the subject. You show up in town, no room booked, beguile both me and my daughter, wander the streets at odd hours…you are a mystery. So tell me, what are these talents of yours? And should I suspect that they're the reason you're here?"

Yikes, but he was perceptive. That did *not* bode well for me.

"Suppose you're right…why would I tell you?" I asked.

He shifted, turning toward me. Though he didn't bridge the space between us, the move felt intimate nonetheless. My heart pattered, pulse racing. I wore his robe and little else.

"Because you want to." His voice turned husky and low.

"I don't trust anyone." I said it mostly to remind myself. "Why would I trust a man I'd just met?"

He leaned back, resting his hand against the side of his head. "You already trust me. And I think, for some reason, I trust you. I let a stranger into my home—the home I share with my daughter. And you entered a strange man's home and donned his robe. For some reason, either we both trust each other, or we're both losing our marbles."

"I vote for the latter."

He smirked and took a sip of his tea. "Fair enough."

Silence stretched. I ate a few more helpings from the tray of delectable treats, even snatching a chocolate truffle from a bowl on the table.

"When I first saw you in my store, I thought you were a figment of my imagination," he confessed.

That earned a short, sharp laugh. "What? The little pixie with the green hair?" I laughed again as a faint tinge of pink flared in his ruddy complexion. "Do my eyes deceive me, or does he blush?"

He chuckled, the sound hearty but not so booming as to wake the sleeping Kenzie. "It was everything. How peaceful you looked. So content. My… I know it's taboo, talking about this, but let's just say there was someone else once—Kenzie's mom—and I never felt like enough. She thought our marriage would be different. A posh apartment in Manhattan and hobnobbing with the literary elite. That we'd be swimming in cash, jet-setting to conferences in London or Paris. And the reality." He gestured to the apartment. "It's this. I love books. I sell books. I make a modest living. I live in a town that I love, that's a safe place to raise my daughter."

I stared at the dregs in the bottom of my mug. Because I'd almost turned his life's dream and his safe haven into a crime scene. True, not a gruesome one, but my stomach felt like I'd just swallowed lead.

If Magnus noticed my reaction, he didn't say. He bridged the distance between us, seizing my hand. "I could tell, when I saw you, that you could see that. That's why I trusted you, I think. On sight. I could see you liked the quiet of it, the quiet comfort of a good book. You were so beautiful. I'd wanted so much to ask you if you were new to town, to ask you out for a cup of coffee or dinner. I didn't expect to see you again."

His thumb swept over my palm, and my heartbeat skittered. How could such a simple move nearly undo me?

Our eyes locked. His other hand moved up to cup my face.

Every cell in my body quivered. Oh, I wanted so much more than a kiss.

"Magnus…" His name dripped from my lips, containing the spark of desire that I knew, together, we could stoke into a full-fledged flame of passion.

Even if only for one night.

Would that be so wrong?

"Can I kiss you, Juniper?" He angled my chin toward his waiting lips.

"Please." The word came out desperate, but I didn't have time to care.

Because his lips seized mine, and all else fell away. He tasted like tea and sugar, a hint of spice. His fingers tangled in my hair, and I returned the favor, drawing him in deeper.

I climbed into his lap, straddling him. Little more than a couple of layers of flimsy fabric separated us. I could tell he wanted me. I moaned, arching against him.

With a groan, he drew away.

"I can't." His eyes darted toward the hallway.

"Right. Kenzie."

What had I almost done?

I wasn't just losing my touch as a thief. I was losing my mind. Every last brain cell. *Whoosh*. Vanished.

I slid off his lap, readjusting the robe—his robe. "I should probably go."

"You can stay, Juniper. There's more snow heading this way, and you can't just wander the streets."

Right. I rubbed my amulet, the emerald gemstone's magic gone quiet. Slowly, I nodded. I was trapped in Mount Holly. I didn't know for how long. The amulet had never failed me before, after all.

I plopped back down on the sofa with a sigh.

Magnus held out the plate of shortbread, and I couldn't help the laugh. "Where did you learn to make such good shortbread?"

"Believe it or not, it's a family recipe, passed down through the generations."

I bit into a piece, buttery and crumbly. "You bake the world's best shortbread, and you own a bookstore. How is it some bookworm hasn't snatched you up?"

He leaned back, resting his head on his elbow. "No, you don't. It's your turn. I've told you my tragic tale."

"There's nothing to tell." I turned away from his prying gaze.

"Tell me about your necklace. The setting is unusual."

"You know jewelry?" The more I learned about the man, the more I wanted to learn—layers upon layers, waiting to be explored.

He shook his head. "Not particularly. My mother collects antique pieces, and I've picked up a bit of knowledge trailing after her at estate sales."

"Ah. Well, it's a one of a kind, as far as I know. The stone is a rare form of emerald, actually." Truthfully, it was a type of crystal found only in the Faerie Realm, one fashioned into a magical amulet that allowed me to transport myself. But I couldn't very well tell Magnus *that*.

"It means something to you, though."

"Yes." I shifted, uncomfortable as he waited. Finally, I sighed. I held the amulet out for him to examine. "It represents freedom. The ability to come and go as I please, where I please, when I please."

"Mysterious." He waggled his eyebrows. "You are truly a woman of intrigue. Tell me, who gave you this bauble?"

"My stepfather…acquired it for me." My stomach soured as I said the words. That was the day he'd turned me into a criminal—just like him. He'd found it in a cache of stolen goods.

With your abilities, just imagine what you can do. And when I said no, he'd taken my locket—the last relic of my mother—and sold it. He'd berated me and tormented me until I agreed.

Who could I have been?

Magnus slid closer. "He mistreated you." The words weren't a question but a statement.

My throat was parched. "What makes you say that?"

He reached up to brush a solitary tear off my cheek. "I'm so sorry that happened to you, Juniper. You're safe here, tonight."

I studied him. A fervent honesty filled his gaze. This was a good man. A man who thought deeply, who loved his daughter, who treated others with decency.

And I was so far from what he deserved.

"I'm a thief," I blurted out. The words escaped before I could stop them.

I don't know what he had expected me to say, but it obviously wasn't that.

He leapt up, banging his shin against the coffee table so hard he cursed. "A thief?" he repeated.

I nodded. I stood and went to the window, staring at the quiet street below. "I don't know why you trust me. I don't know why anyone here even notices me. I tend to get in, get out without anyone being the wiser. I've learned to be invisible. I've learned to be alone."

He stared at me, his face, for once, unreadable.

"A thief, Magnus. A thief," I repeated, needing the word to sink in.

On the street below, a snow truck passed by, the sound of the plow scraping against asphalt as it went.

I turned back to see him rubbing his newly bruised shin.

"That's why you're here, then." His gaze narrowed. "What? Who?"

Two simple words.

And an answer that would ruin the magic of the night.

"I was sent here to steal a book." I met his eyes, readying myself for the betrayal, the disdain, the contempt I would soon see there.

I sucked in a deep breath.

"You," I answered his second question. "I was sent here to rob you."

Chapter Five

Magnus frowned. He stepped around the sofa, almost seeming to put himself between me and the hallway—protecting Kenzie, no doubt.

"I would never, ever hurt your daughter," I assured him. "I don't hurt people. That's not what I do."

"You steal from people, though."

"Bad people. I steal…" I sighed. "No. I'm tired. I'm tired of justifying it. The truth is they pay me, and I do their bidding."

He narrowed his eyes, the brown deepening from warm chocolate to coffee without so much as a drop of cream. "Whose bidding?"

I snorted. "You wouldn't believe me if I told you."

He crossed the room in wide strides. He was tall, and I was suddenly aware of my short stature. He towered over me, demanding answers.

"I invited you into my home, Juniper. Where my daughter is asleep. Are you joking? Making this up? You think it's funny?"

"Nothing about this is funny," I snapped. "It's not a joke."

"Tell me the truth," he growled. I didn't think he was the sort who got angry often.

"It would be easier if I showed you."

I was still clad in his robe and Kenzie's playfully patterned socks, but at that moment, I didn't care. Before

I could second guess what I was about to do, I opened the door and headed downstairs, toward the back room of the bookstore and the safe I'd spotted earlier that day.

"Juniper!" Magnus huffed after me as I went. "June," he hissed again.

Downstairs, I twisted the knob to the office of the bookstore, but it didn't turn.

He leaned against the bottom of the banister, crossing his arms. "It's locked."

"Watch," I said.

What I was about to do violated a dozen or so rules of the fae—and a few dozen rules of the magical community in general—when dealing with non-magical humans. Mortals.

But I wanted Magnus to know, to understand. Why, I wasn't sure. I couldn't bring myself to board that train of thought.

I held my hand out so my palm hovered a couple of inches from the brass doorknob. And then I unleashed my magic.

Green wisps of magic flickered around my palm, like emerald-hued flames. They encircled the doorknob, finding their way into the locking mechanism.

It clicked open mere seconds later with a subtle pop.

I let the magic dissipate and then twisted the knob again. This time, it turned easily at my touch.

"Voila," I said, deadpan.

The spell cast, I turned to him. What would I see on his face? Fear? Contempt? Panic?

"Did you just…?" His voice trailed off as he gestured at the now-open door.

"Yup. If you think that was wild, want to see me crack the safe?"

I flipped on the light inside the office. It revealed the safe, an old, weathered rolltop desk, a couple of metal file cabinets, and a small console table with an electric tea kettle surrounded by assorted mugs and tea tins.

Magnus peered at me, but he didn't seem angry anymore. "You're what, some sort of witch?"

I shook my head. "No. Witches are human. I'm a faerie."

His eyes widened. "I guess all those stories my uncle told me as a kid are true, then. Or all those cookies are giving me some weird-ass dreams. Maybe I shouldn't have eaten one of Marjory Waxman's devil's-food-cake cookies."

I held up my hands, letting my magic coalesce in my palms where it formed swirling green orbs. "You're not dreaming, Magnus. But if you want, I know a wizard who could make you think this was all a dream. Your choice."

He stared at me, his lips partially open. "A faerie," he repeated.

I nodded. "Sent to steal a book—a spellbook, actually."

His brows knitted together. "A spellbook? Why would I have…?" Realization dawned on his face. "That rascal."

He brushed past me, turning the dial on the safe until the door popped open. He reached inside and pulled out a book with a weathered, brownish-red cover. He brushed the cover off in a move that must've been more muscle memory than necessity. He gazed down at the cover, those wrinkles in his brow deepening.

"This, you mean? Is this the book you were sent here to steal?"

I looked at it. *The Witch's Hearth: Spells, Potions, and Remedies for the Cottage Witch.* "It has to be."

"Why would anyone send you to steal it? It's nothing but some old folk remedies. It's a gorgeous book, but nothing…" He trailed off, as if another thought had dawned on him. "You're a faerie. So someone magical sent you here to get this?"

I nodded.

"Another faerie?"

I shook my head.

"A witch!" he guessed. Judging by his playful tone, he still didn't think this was serious. Maybe he thought my magic was a fancy illusion, something out of a Vegas magician's show. Or maybe he really was convinced this was all a dream.

"A wizard," I supplied.

"Hmm…I didn't see that one coming." He turned away from me, muttering, "But that would explain a lot."

I took the book from his hands. I felt no darkness in its magic, no hint of shadow, no vague stench of sulfur to suggest some vileness lurking within its pages.

I frowned at him over the top of the book, which appeared to be filled with nothing more than the folk remedies he had mentioned. The author even discussed using a raw potato to cure warts and a recipe for a honey and rosemary tonic to soothe a sore throat.

Magnus looked on, then raked a hand through his hair and gave a heavy sigh.

"What's wrong?" I asked.

"I wanted this night to be real." The longing in those words cut me deeper than any blade ever could.

Ah. So he'd settled on the it's-all-some-crazy-dream scenario as the most logical.

I set the book aside. A growing list of questions formed in my brain, one of which was why a wizard as powerful as Oliver sent a renowned faerie thief to steal a book that was, on its surface, worthless. And I was a thief—a magical thief. I knew when I was stealing rubbish.

I seized Magnus's hand, drawing him toward me. My lips curled into a playful smile, hands sliding up his arms to cup his cheeks. "We could make some very amazing memories, at least."

Truth be told, I knew I couldn't stay. Mount Holly might have possessed its own unique magic, but its magic and mine simply didn't mix. And what scenario could I create in which I retired from a life of thievery to settle into a quaint small town?

"Juniper." His voice was husky as it caressed each syllable. "I think I would like that very much—the memory of you."

He brought his lips to mine. Nothing in his kiss was tentative.

I groaned.

He meant to devour me.

I meant to let him.

If I only got to spend one night with Magnus MacDougal, I'd make the most of it.

I opened my mouth to his. He gave a hungry moan as the kiss deepened. I arched against him, his erection plain against the fabric of his pajamas.

He cupped my buttocks, tugging me against him. I writhed, an ache pulsing at the apex of my legs.

If I'd had a plan, it went right out the window when he picked me up and set me on the edge of the desk. He untied the robe, his fingers clumsy, and pushed the terry fabric away from my shoulders.

"You're beautiful, June." He took my nipples in his mouth, first one, then the other, his hands cupping and squeezing my breasts while he licked and sucked. I clenched his shoulders, then the edge of the desk, straining against him.

He parted my legs, fingering me through my panties. They were tiny scraps of lace, a luxury I allowed myself but usually kept hidden. I'd chosen bright red when I dressed—it was the Christmas season, after all.

He didn't bother to slide the scrap of lace down my legs. The flimsy panties tore easily, and he tossed them aside.

I giggled.

"I'll buy you a new pair," he growled.

I giggled again, the sound freeing. "No need. I have plenty more where those came from," I promised.

"Mmm," he growled again.

I kissed him, running my fingers through his hair. I wanted to savor this moment with him, remember every second even as my body begged for release.

I stood and kissed his neck while my fingers worked the buttons on his clothes.

"I can—" he started, but I stopped him with a kiss.

"I want to," I whispered in his ear.

His groan, a mixture of frustration and pleasure, nearly undid me. I forced myself to go slowly. When he wore only his boxer shorts—which were seasonally appropriate, complete with candy canes—I wrapped my hand around him.

Any thought of going slowly vanished. He moved his hand between my legs and slid not one, but two fingers inside of me.

He set me on the desk again, and this time I opened to him. He eased himself inside.

I leaned my head back as he thrust, again and again. I couldn't take my gaze off his face, eyes half-closed in ecstasy, dark hair framing that square jawline.

The pleasure built until it reached a crescendo. I let myself fall over the edge and felt him shiver in his own release.

In the moment that followed, I caught another glimpse of his aura. Like before, it had hints of sky blue and cobalt, royal blue and turquoise. But now, mixed in, were streaks of vibrant spring green.

Amid the swirling shades of green, my own aura now shimmered with wisps of sky blue.

And that was definitely new. The sharing of aura magic was a first for me, for sure.

I was too tired to wonder what that newfound magic meant. I leaned my head against his shoulder, and he wrapped his arms around me, planting kisses in my hair.

"That was magical," he whispered.

I nuzzled his shoulder and settled my head into a comfortable spot. "You have no idea."

****

I woke up in a sea of warm flannel sheets, under a downy comforter, sunlight streaming in through a window.

I stirred and sat up. I wore Magnus's robe, and the memory of last night swept over me. At some point, we'd dressed, and he'd quietly carried me into his bedroom.

I glanced at the bedside clock. Eight a.m. The sound of voices down the hall told me Magnus and Kenzie were already awake.

My clothes were freshly laundered, neatly folded,

and resting on a bench at the foot of the bed. The room was masculine and a bit formal but still had a cozy, inviting air about it. A gray down comforter over dark green sheets. Vintage maps secured in walnut frames hung on blue-gray walls. The four-poster bed matched a chest of drawers and end tables, and a black-and-white checkered armchair with a "merry and bright" throw pillow sat in the corner.

I glanced out the window. The shops were dark on Christmas morning, but the town still felt, well, merry. And bright. Sunlight sparkled off untouched snow.

My lips curved upward in a smile.

Magnus was…

No. He was an amazing man who, as soon as I got the amulet's magic fixed, I wouldn't see again. Simple as that.

I tugged my shirt on and tucked the amulet underneath, its magic sleeping and still. I opened the door quietly and stepped into the bathroom across the hall, butterflies rising in my stomach again.

Wow. Man, what were they doing? Some sort of butterfly acrobatics in there?

I didn't know what to do. I couldn't leave the apartment without encountering Magnus and Kenzie. I wasn't sure how he felt about last night. If he had thought it was all a dream, he must've been shocked this morning to find me asleep in his bed.

And Kenzie? I felt like a jerk. She was a sweet kid, and she didn't need some woman coming in and messing up her life.

After I'd brushed my hair way more than necessary, I steeled what nerve I had left and started down the hall.

Two sets of eyes turned toward me.

Well, three if I counted the cat, a gray tabby with vibrant green eyes. Her ears twitched as she caught the scent of my magic. Cats were good at that—they always knew when a faerie was nearby.

Kenzie jumped up. "Dad said we had to wait for you to open presents," she huffed, but she didn't sound annoyed—merely impatient.

I glanced at Magnus. "That's not necessary. I should actually…"

He cleared his throat. "I told Kenzie about the problem at the McHenry House. How they'd double-booked guests and you couldn't find another room."

Kenzie was rifling through the massive pile of presents under the tree.

"Ah." I was grateful for his quick thinking, though I wondered if she bought that.

She didn't seem to care.

"This one is for you, Luna." Kenzie unwrapped a plastic stocking full of various holiday-themed cat toys.

Luna jumped off her perch on the sofa arm and went over to inspect the gift. Kenzie fished out a toy shaped like a Christmas tree, and the tabby immediately went to town batting it around on the hardwood.

"You next, Dad," Kenzie said with a smile. She handed Magnus—now clad in khakis and a plaid sweater—one of his gifts.

He ever so carefully opened the present, and I wondered if he was the sort of man who saved wrapping paper for reuse.

I wanted to know a lot of things about him, actually.

And the events of the previous night raised questions about a lot of things.

Like, why the amulet stopped working. And why

Oliver had lied to me.

And what if I wanted something different with my life? Could I ever really have a different sort of life?

"Thanks, Kenz," Magnus said as he inspected the gift—a pair of charcoal gray slippers.

She opened a few boxes, containing everything from makeup to clothing to a new cell phone case. "There's one for you, June!" she squealed, seizing a small box and thrusting it at me.

"There is?" My gaze flew to Magnus.

He shrugged. "It's not anything fancy."

My hands shook. I hadn't had a present under the tree on Christmas morning in—well, ages. No Christmases. No birthdays.

I swallowed the lump in my throat and opened the small card taped to the top of the box.

Found this at an estate sale years ago. Never knew why I bought it. Then I met you, and now I know. Merry Christmas, M.

Oh no. The butterflies were back in full force again.

My hands were shaking so badly I could barely tear the paper. I could feel Magnus's gaze boring into me, though Kenzie was, thankfully, distracted by balling up bits of wrapping paper and rolling them toward a waiting Luna.

Inside was a small jewelry box. I flipped the lid open.

Time stood still. Everything else vanished as I looked at the contents of the box.

It was a silver, heart-shaped locket, instantly familiar.

I blinked, trying to get any muscle in my body to work again.

When I glanced up, Magnus was beside me. "May I?"

I could only nod.

With gentle fingers, he took the locket out of the box and opened it. "I never opened it until last night."

Inside, side by side, were two photos. One of my mother, with her bright smile. The other was a younger me, a bit of mischief in my eyes.

He knelt beside me on the floor and fastened the chain around my neck. "Merry Christmas, Juniper," he whispered in my ear.

"Merry Christmas," I whispered back.

He rested his hands on my shoulders. Somehow, he'd given me everything I'd ever wanted. I didn't know how to thank him.

After Kenzie tore through the rest of her gifts and Magnus opened a few more, he started making breakfast—pancakes, sausage, bacon, and fresh fruit—while I helped Kenzie pick up the tattered scraps of wrapping paper littering the living-room floor.

Luna was less than helpful, though she seemed to enjoy batting at our legs while we cleaned.

"You were right, by the way," Kenzie said as we worked. "About Luna. She didn't seem to mind the dark at all. When we got back, she was just staring out the window, watching the snow."

"I'm glad to hear it." I tossed another cat toy in Luna's direction, laughing as she lay on her back, grasped the toy in her front paws, and kicked it furiously with her back legs.

A knock at the door interrupted the conversation.

"I'll get it!" Kenzie said. "Who's there?" Her hand hovered over the doorknob.

"Your favorite uncle," a male voice replied.

I backed up so quickly I nearly knocked over an end table. The lamp wobbled, coming dangerously close to toppling over.

I knew that voice.

Wait. Uncle?

Kenzie didn't hesitate. She flung open the door and wrapped her arms around the man waiting on the other side. "Uncle Oliver!"

The gift bags of various sizes he'd been carrying tumbled to the floor, but he didn't seem to mind, just gave a hearty laugh in response and wrapped her in a bear hug.

Familiar blue eyes met mine, lips curling into a smile. "I trust you've had a pleasant stay in Mount Holly, my dear?" Oliver asked.

"I…" I glanced at Magnus in the kitchen.

"Uncle Oliver." Magnus wiped his hands on a tea towel. "I wasn't expecting you."

"Oh, you know me," Oliver said. "Full of surprises and all that. Walter wanted to come check on the horses, so here we are."

"I…" I swallowed, searching for words. No. Oliver had tricked me. And I needed to know why.

As if sensing my consternation, he glanced at me. "Magnus, you get to work on what smells like a delightful breakfast. I do believe an old acquaintance and I have some catching up to do."

He winked at Kenzie. "No peeking in those bags until I get back, young lady," he said as he held the door open for me.

What else could I do?

I grabbed my jacket and followed the old wizard out into the cold.

Chapter Six

Oliver was dressed in human clothes—a long navy coat with a pin-striped suit underneath. His long white beard grazed his red plaid scarf, and his eyes twinkled as he waved to a young couple across the street.

We walked to the town square where Oliver discreetly magicked away the snow on a park bench.

I plopped down, arms crossed over my chest, and angled myself toward him. "Answers," I growled. "Now."

The wizard chuckled, obviously not the least bit fazed by the annoyance in my tone. "I've known you for many years, Juniper. You were what, nineteen years old when I first hired you?"

I shrugged. That was shortly before my stepfather had been arrested—one of our last jobs together, actually. "I believe so."

He settled against the bench. "You were a lost soul then—angry at the entire world. And for a long time after. But over the past year, I've watched your anger change into something else. You've been lonely, my dear, living a life someone else chose for you. If you could have anything, what would it be?"

"What are you, Santa Claus?"

He gave a hearty chuckle, his hand coming to his belly. "Definitely not. Though he is a member of the Order of Magicks, believe it or not."

"I don't know *what* to believe anymore. You sent me here to steal a worthless book you said contained dangerous magic that could destroy the world. From an innocent man trying to run a business and raise his daughter…from your own nephew?" I tried to rein in my temper, restrain myself from yelling—or worse, from hoisting the wizard up by his collar.

"I will answer your questions." He remained unflappably calm in the face of my outburst. "But first, answer mine. Close your eyes, pause, and listen. What do you want?"

I'd never dared to ask myself such a question. Both in the Faerie Realm and the magical community here on earth, I'd always felt I had to keep up my reputation as a thief. At least it offered me some sort of reputation in the magical community—and although being a thief wasn't exactly a respected profession, it was an in-demand one among magical types.

But I did as Oliver asked. I settled into a comfortable position on the bench and closed my eyes.

What do I want?

Well, I wanted those pancakes Magnus was whipping up. A smile curled my lips as I pictured him flipping flapjacks up in the air in his Christmas sweater. Heat pulled at the apex of my legs as I recalled the night we'd shared together.

I wanted that—sleeping curled up with him, sharing family pancake breakfasts. I wanted summer picnics and autumn apple picking. And I wanted Christmas mornings.

But I didn't deserve it. Not yet. I had to make changes.

My eyelids fluttered open, the winter sky a vibrant

blue, the snow dazzling in the morning sunlight. "I want a fresh start. I want a chance to be the kind of woman that Magnus could…"

I couldn't bring myself to finish the words.

"Say it," Oliver said, his voice paternal but not patronizing.

"Love," I whispered.

"Ah." He stroked his beard. "I thought you might. Well, I didn't see it at first. It was Walter, actually, who first spotted it. He's a bit of a matchmaker, that husband of mine."

I snorted. "That doesn't surprise me. But why on earth would he think Magnus and I…?"

He shrugged. "Walter has his ways. *They need each other,* he said. I think he saw that Magnus—and Mount Holly—could give you something you desperately needed without knowing it."

I narrowed my gaze. "So you sent me to rob him on Christmas Eve?"

"Would you have come voluntarily without such a ruse?" he countered.

Even I had to laugh. "Okay, fair point. What about the book?"

He waved this off. "A decoy. It's been in my library at my farm here in Mount Holly for years. A fascinating read, but no dangerous magical secrets."

"Uh-huh." My thoughts strayed to the thunder-snow the night before—the freak snowstorm no one had predicted—and my amulet's sudden power outage. "You didn't cast a little spell last night, did you?"

"Ah. No." His eyes twinkled. "That was Walter. My dear husband thought you needed a little push. I thought it was unnecessary. He used a bit too much oomph in that one, though—knocked the power out to most of town."

He stood and offered me his arm. I accepted, looping mine through his.

We began to walk back toward Magnus's apartment.

With each step, my heart pounded more and more, my blood a roar in my ears. "I don't have any skills beyond—well, you know. What use is a bit of faerie magic in a town full of humans?"

"None whatsoever, my dear," he assured me, his tone frustratingly calm. "But do you like horses?"

"I guess. Never thought about it. Why?"

He shrugged and opened the back door to the building, one that led to a set of stairs to Magnus's apartment. "Walter and I have a guest cottage at our farm, and we could use another stable hand. It's a normal, boring job, but the cottage is snug and cozy, and we'd pay you well."

We'd arrived at the door to Magnus's apartment, but I couldn't bring myself to enter.

"What if…?" Did I dare utter the words? "If he doesn't…?"

Oliver reached out and squeezed my arm. The smile on his face was soft and gentle. "Trust me, my dear. He does."

****

Wow. Magnus was an amazing cook.

We were drinking tea in the living room post-breakfast, a fire crackling in the fireplace while Oliver regaled us with a tale of the time he and Walter had fended off a werewolf attack and helped a recently turned werewolf learn to control his newfound abilities.

Even the cat, Luna, sat at attention, not daring to so much as lick a paw or bat a Christmas ornament while the wizard told his story.

"And he's okay now?" Kenzie asked. "Like, he's not going to eat his family or anything?"

"Kenzie, that tale took place thirty-seven years ago, and that freshly turned wolf is now a member of parliament." He seemed to consider this. "Although I'm not really sure whether that means he's *okay*. But he did learn to master his abilities."

He reached out to set his empty mug on the coffee table. "Well, I must get back to my devoted husband. I think we bought out every carrot at the grocery store for the horses."

Kenzie's eyes lit up. She glanced at her father. "Dad, I know it's Christmas, but can I go with? I want to see Uncle Walter and meet the new horse. His name is Percival. Right, Uncle Oliver?"

"Indeed. Percy is quite the gentleman, too. Hasn't thrown me off once. Though he did give the farrier a run for her money when she came to shoe him recently."

Magnus sighed. "Make sure she's back before four. We have a dinner date," he reminded them.

Oliver gave Magnus a bear hug and a pat on the back. When he hugged me, he whispered, "Whenever you're ready, the guest cottage at Excalibur Farms is waiting."

Kenzie gave Magnus a hug and me a little wave, then slid into her jacket and boots and followed Oliver out the door.

I swallowed and turned to Magnus.

"I should start the dishwasher before I forget." He turned away to do just that.

"Do you want me to go?" I blurted out. I didn't expect to feel this way, and my feet wanted to run, run fast and run far and keep running forever.

But my heart?

My heart wanted to be here, in this moment, with Magnus.

He glanced at me and frowned as he pressed a few buttons on the dishwasher. "Do you want to go?"

I could only shake my head.

He crossed the room, swept me off my feet, and kissed me.

Afterward, entangled with him in the sheets, I traced my fingers along his chest, memorizing the contours of his body.

"Last night, you thought I was a dream," I reminded him.

He gazed down at me. "I'm glad you weren't."

"But what about…everything? The fact that I am—well, I was—a thief. And a faerie. Can you handle all of that?"

"Uncle Oliver told me about your stepfather while you and Kenzie were cleaning up after breakfast. Someone used you, and then you didn't feel you had a choice." He brushed my hair away from my face, toying with the green strands. "Now you have a choice."

I smiled, warmed by the comfort of his touch, the fondness in his chocolate eyes. "Oliver offered me a job at the farm," I told him. "A chance to make an honest living, to see if there's a place for me here in Mount Holly."

His hand trailed down my side, coming to rest on my hip. "Have you decided what you'll do?"

I brought my hands to his chest. Beneath my touch, his breath quickened. My own did as well.

I nodded. "I'm going to stay, Magnus. I want to see

where this goes."

He grinned. "I hoped you'd say that."

He kissed me senseless, then nuzzled my neck.

"Merry Christmas, Juniper Whitethorn," he muttered against my ear. He nuzzled me again before leaning back against his pillow and tucking me into his side. "The faerie thief who stole my heart."

Secret
Family Recipes
for Love
and
Butter Cookies

by

Melissa McTernan

Christmas Cookies

Dedication

To Josie,
for her butter cookie recipe
and hundreds of happy Christmas memories

Chapter One

Christmas Eve, Present Day, New Hampshire

Bea stood in the middle of the kitchen, floured hands on her apron-covered hips, and surveyed the damage. Old cookbooks, recipe cards, and ladies' magazine clippings from the last thirty years littered every surface. Her first batch of cookies cooled on the last square foot of space on the kitchen island and another batch filled the oven. Despite her best efforts, none of them seemed right. She had to find that recipe.

She turned, arms akimbo, toward Camille, her best friend since the dawn of time. Camille sat at the kitchen island, head on the counter, in a cookie-induced coma.

"Magic Christmas cookies don't make themselves you know." In fact, Bea worried they might not exist at all.

"Are you going to help me?" She wiped her hands on the Santa face covering the front of her apron and huffed a small sigh of frustration.

Camille lifted her head. "Are you kidding? I've been helping you all afternoon." Her glare and menacing tone were hard to take seriously with the recipe card stuck to her forehead.

Bea stifled a laugh and pulled it off to read it before apologizing. "You're right. I'm sorry. I wanted everything to go perfectly, and now I can't remember which cookie is the magic cookie."

The magic cookie had made countless generations of her family members fall madly in love. It was a family tradition. If only she had paid closer attention to the stories.

Asking her parents or her brother for the recipe was out of the question. It didn't seem Christmas appropriate to say, "So I want to make Aiden—the man we've all essentially adopted as one of our own—fall passionately in love with me, and if he hoists me onto this counter and has his way with me right here in the kitchen, then all the better."

Camille gave her a grim smile as she sorted through the recipes, tossing out anything that wasn't Christmas-related.

"Explain to me again what we're looking for," she said, brushing off the closest card. "Will the recipe say magic Christmas cookies that make people fall in love, or do they have a catchier title?"

"Ha. Ha. I wish it were that easy."

Camille ran a hand down her arm and gave her a squeeze. "I don't want you to be disappointed. Again."

Bea pasted on her bravest smile. "I won't be disappointed because this is the year." *Did you hear that Universe? This year will be the year.* She returned to flipping through her mother's cookbooks.

"What makes you think after spending the last ten Christmases with Aiden this will be the year he realizes he loves you?" Camille asked as she opened an ancient magazine. The glossy paper had absorbed too many spills over the years and protested loudly as Camille continued to search. Each turn of a page sounded more like stomping on dry leaves than browsing for recipes.

"I'm turning twenty-five in five days. By every definition of the word, I will be a grown-ass adult. And this Christmas I will finally get Aiden McLean to see me as more than his best friend's little sister if it kills me."

Never mind that she had said this same thing since the year she turned twenty. There's no difference between twenty and twenty-three, she had said. And every year since she waited for Aiden to see her as something more, to take her seriously, to forget he had known her since she was fifteen, and to notice her now as someone new.

"Piece of cake." Camille flipped another rejected recipe into the pile.

"Or cookies, as the case may be."

****

An hour later, a small stack of contenders sat in Bea's magic love cookie pile, and several plates were full of her first efforts. Her mission to try every recipe was well underway.

Camille gave her a kiss on the cheek. "Try not to eat all of these while I'm gone." Camille's family also had a house on the lake and they joined Bea's family every year for Christmas Eve dinner. She'd be back later with her parents and sisters in tow.

Bea tucked the recipes in a cookbook for low-calorie meals, the perfect hiding place, and put the baking ingredients in the cabinets. She gently piled the cookies into a tin from her mother's ever-expanding collection and wiped the counters.

Satisfied with her efforts, she stirred the marinara sauce bubbling on the stove. Thankfully, even in the midst of her cookie mania, she had remembered to start it. The tangy, savory smell was the perfect antidote to her afternoon of cookie testing. She lifted the spoon, tasted, added a pinch of salt, and congratulated herself on at least accomplishing one culinary task today.

She glanced at the clock, half-hidden behind the garland her father hung around every doorway. It was late. Hopefully, her mother was on her way home by now. Someone needed to boil the lobsters. The sauce was one thing, but lobsters were an entirely different matter. A matter that required her mother.

Somewhere along the line, Bea's family dropped several of the fishes in the Feast of the Seven Fishes tradition in Italian families, but she enjoyed their watered-down version just as much. Linguine with shrimp and lobster tails was her idea of a perfect Christmas Eve dinner.

She finished in the kitchen and took a spin around the living room, straightening the multitude of holiday pillows. The room was spacious, separated from the kitchen by the massive island, decorated somewhere between rustic-chic holiday and craft store explosion. Between the overstuffed sofa and love seat, and what might have been their biggest Christmas tree yet, the room seemed smaller than usual.

She turned on the tree lights and stuck her face near the branches, breathing deep. The sharp pine scent immediately brought memories to mind: running down the stairs to tear open her presents every year, wanting nothing but a white Christmas the year she turned eight, and, of course, the Christmas her brother brought home the man of her dreams. Bea sighed. She wasn't a gawky teenager crushing on her brother's friend anymore. All she needed to do now was convince Aiden it was true.

Her gaze landed on Aiden's stocking hanging over

the fireplace, his name scrawled in glitter across the top like the rest of the family's. After several years of spending Christmas here, they insisted he have a matching stocking. She traced the letters of his name with her finger, remembering the look on his face when they gave it to him. He had ducked his head, rubbing a hand over the back of his neck, the way he did when he was embarrassed, and quickly thanked her parents, wanting them to move on to the next present.

She loved the way Aiden's name looked next to hers. It looked right. Their names belonged together. They belonged together.

She stepped back, admiring the lights twinkling through the fake snow surrounding the Christmas village sitting on top of the mantel. Everything was ready.

Bea glanced outside at the darkening sky. The sunset spilled pink on the clouds. Christmas Eve anticipation fluttered in her stomach. Waiting for everyone to arrive was half the fun. Her father was last-minute shopping, enjoying the rush of working under pressure. Her brother, James, and his fiancé, Alex, were driving in from Connecticut today. And Aiden promised to be here before dinner.

She preferred Christmas Eve to Christmas Day. It was the sweet spot in between waiting all December for the big day, and the moment on Christmas night when you realized it was all over and had gone by so fast. On Christmas Eve, you existed in that delicious moment of waiting and wondering and hoping. There was no disappointment on Christmas Eve, no forgotten gifts, no overstuffed bellies, no torn wrapping paper. There was only hope.

Bea wandered to her room to shower and dress,

running her hand across the wood-paneled walls as she went, the grooves tickling her fingers. All her happiest memories had happened within these walls, in this cabin in the woods. And this year she hoped to add the happiest memory of all. She and Aiden together. It was the one thing she wanted for Christmas.

****

Aiden pulled into the driveway at the Millers' lake house, his tires crunching over the gravel. He took a deep breath, steeling himself. Judging by the parked cars, he beat James again this year. The white lights lining the roof twinkled merrily and puffs of smoke trailed from the chimney. The scene was so postcard-perfect he almost scoffed. But this was the one place he considered home. He would never mock it, not even alone in his car.

He grabbed his overnight bag from the backseat and made his way over the icy path toward the front door. Bea pulled it open before he reached the top porch step. The jingle bells on the wreath rang his welcome.

She stood framed in the doorway, her blonde hair like a halo around her round face. She grinned from ear to ear, and his heart stuttered in his chest. No one else looked at him like that.

"Aiden! You're here." She wound her arms around him before he uttered a word. Her vanilla-scented warmth assaulted him.

"Bea, hey." He squirmed, keeping his voice neutral even as his heart hammered against his ribcage. He hadn't made it past the threshold yet and it was already too much. She was too much. Bea eased back, gazing up at him, and he was forced to discover for the millionth time the intensity of her blue eyes and the brightness of her radiant smile.

"Merry Christmas. I missed you."

"Merry Christmas," he mumbled, trying and failing to untangle himself from this attack of love and cheer. Surviving a week was sure to be torture. Torture inflicted by the beautiful woman running her hands down his back and sending shivers up his spine that had nothing to do with the cold.

Whether she meant it to be or not, Bea's crush on him was obvious. She didn't so much wear her heart on her sleeve as let it shine through her smile. But she was off-limits. A fact he tried desperately to remember while he was wrapped in her arms.

"James! Alex! Merry Christmas!" The arrival of her brother and his fiancé pulled Bea's attention away from Aiden. He sighed with relief at the diversion and hurried to help them with their packages. The men trudged up the driveway, each with armloads of presents, their smiling faces peeking from behind the precarious towers.

Aiden took the opportunity to sneak into the house and left Bea to her family reunion. He loved the week every Christmas at the cabin with the Millers, but it was harder and harder to ignore Bea's feelings for him. God, and that hug. Her body was imprinted on his, and despite everything, he wanted to keep it there.

He pushed open the door, presents in one arm, duffle bag slung over the other. The house was quiet when he walked in except for the faint sound of an upbeat pop song drifting in from the kitchen. It was Bea's favorite Christmas song. If she were in here right now, she would be singing it at the top of her horribly off-key lungs. His mouth twitched, wanting to smile, but he pressed his lips together. Finding her adorable was not an option.

"Aiden, how was the trip?" Bea's father, Cole,

bustled in from the kitchen sporting a Ho, Ho, Ho printed apron and an aggressively patterned Christmas sweater underneath.

Aiden smiled then. Cole, as he insisted Aiden call him, was one of his favorite people. The man's enthusiasm for the holidays was contagious.

"Not bad at all. Merry Christmas." He placed the heap of presents on the kitchen island. James had gone overboard again.

Aiden turned to Cole in time to be pulled into a tight hug that rivaled the one he just received from Bea. "Merry Christmas. We're so happy all you kids can still make the trip."

"Of course. Wouldn't miss it."

"Is that Aiden I hear?" Bea's mom was not far behind her husband. While Cole was over the top, Fran was understated in her holiday cheer. She wore a simple red sweater and slacks, and of course her traditional dangly jingle bell earrings.

"Hey, Fran. Merry Christmas." Another hug. It was more hugs than Aiden gave in an entire year, but for the people who let him crash their holiday, he allowed it. And maybe even liked it.

"Look at you." She held him tight by the arms, studying him. "Look at him, Cole."

What would it have been like to grow up with a mother who looked at him with such affection? He shook the thought from his mind. No point in going down that road.

"I'm looking, dear." Cole grinned.

Fran released her grip and smiled; something in her expression told him he'd passed her inspection. "You're still as handsome as the day we met you. Any nice girls catch your eye yet?"

"Uh, nobody to report." It was the same every year, this little interview. Luckily, her biological son bustled through the door and cut the interrogation short.

"We're here," James announced, his fingers intertwined with his fiancé's. Aiden ignored the twinge of jealousy working its way into his heart at seeing them together. Not that he wanted James, but he envied their faith in each other, their confidence in their decision to be together. He was tired of showing up here alone.

"Aiden, this is Alex." Aiden reached out a hand, but Alex pulled him in for a hug. Already part of the family.

"I'm so happy to finally meet you." Alex squeezed him tighter. "James's best friend. I feel like I already know you."

"I'm glad to meet you too." Aiden squirmed free from the smaller man's grasp. James beamed at them both.

Bea and her mother had gone off to the kitchen to stir the sauce, or murder lobsters, or something like that, while her father arranged the presents under the Rockefeller-sized tree standing in the great room. It was reflected in the floor-to-ceiling windows overlooking the frozen lake, giving the impression there were two enormous trees towering over them.

"So, James tells me you're an artist."

Aiden ducked his head and ran a hand along the back of his neck. "He exaggerates. I'm a bartender." He served drinks to make money and painted to get out of his own head. He wasn't an artist, but James always introduced him as one.

"He's an amazing painter and don't let him tell you any different." James pointed a scolding finger at him.

He had the same blue eyes as his sister, but his hair was darker and his face slimmer. He had ditched the eyebrow ring and the crush he had on Aiden years ago, but when they were together it was like freshman year all over again. James had always been his number one fan.

"I'm going to drop my bag in my room."

"Good. I'm going to make cocktails."

Aiden let out a laugh on his way to the guest room. James's holiday sangria was enough to put the most seasoned drinkers under the table.

He tossed his bag on the bed and looked around the tidy room. He needed a minute before reentering the festivities. The room had been his since his first trip to the cabin with James ten years ago. The white bedspread with red poinsettias and the toy nutcrackers gracing the top of the dresser were far from his usual taste, but somehow this place was as much his home as his studio apartment in the city.

Laughter erupted from down the hall. Apparently, the drinking had already begun. He opened his bag and put his clothes in the dresser, bracing himself for the evening. He loved these people, but there were a lot of them. And they were loud and touchy. Oh, and he was trying to pretend he didn't have a thing for one of them. It was a lot.

He shoved the empty bag under the bed and ran a hand through his hair. It needed to be cut but he hadn't had the time. The messy strands flopped over his forehead, tickling one of his eyebrows. He pushed it back. The smell of cookies wafted into his room. Butter and sugar conspired to draw him from his hiding place.

He found everyone gathered around the kitchen island.

"Aiden, have a cookie." Bea nearly shoved the tray at him, her eyes twinkling.

Santas, snowmen, stars, and trees covered the platter, all coated in copious amounts of frosting. Bea's grin was blinding as she held out her offering. Aiden snatched a small star and brought it to his lips. The mouthwatering smell of vanilla filled his senses. It was Bea's scent. Her soft blonde curls smelled like vanilla.

His eyes drifted closed as he remembered their hug, the feel of Bea's body molded to his, her hair tickling his face.

"You gonna eat that cookie or make out with it?" Camille's voice broke through his daydream. He nearly choked. What was wrong with him?

She smiled at him as he finally took a bite. Bea leaned forward, watching him chew.

Sprinkles crunched between his teeth. The obscene amount of frosting sent a rush of sugar through his veins. If you could overdose on Christmas, these would be the cookies to do it. Bea waited for a verdict.

"It's delicious."

Camille leaned across the counter, still grinning like he missed the joke. "But would you say they taste magical?"

"Well, since I'm not a leprechaun that lives on the side of a cereal box, no, I would not."

Bea snorted. Sangria sprayed from her mouth. He ignored the warm flush of pride at making her laugh.

Camille tossed her head. Her abundance of black curls fell over one shoulder. "Good one." She gave his arm a playful smack and went to find her sisters by the fireplace.

Bea still giggled next to him, wiping her mouth with

a festive holiday napkin. Christmas covered everything in this cabin. One year he had found holly leaf printed toilet paper in the guest bathroom.

"So…another Christmas…" Aiden leaned against the counter and faced the adjoining living room. James and Alex were cozy together on the love seat. Camille and her two older sisters chatted by the fire. Bea's parents and Camille's parents gestured out the window, discussing the new houses being built around the lake. They were always concerned the lake was becoming overpopulated. "Its isolation and rustic appeal will be lost," Cole had told him on numerous occasions. A downright tragedy.

Bea shifted beside him. Her arm brushed against his. "Yep. Another Christmas."

He struggled for something to say, anything to fill the awkward silence. Anything to distract him from the warmth of her body so close to his.

"You know, we live across the river from each other. It's possible to see each other more often."

The chances of keeping his hands off his best friend's little sister if they weren't surrounded by her entire family were slim at best. The risk was too great.

"Sure, maybe this year." He'd made this promise before. Bea munched another cookie. She was warm and sweet next to him, but he kept his gaze on the room. She overwhelmed his senses as it was, seeing the disappointment on her face might break him. She sighed a little, recognizing the familiar lie.

"Are we on for old movies later?"

It was a tradition to watch classic Christmas movies every year. "Of course," he said, already imagining the darkened room and soft blankets, and Bea curled against him. It might kill him, but sure, why the hell not.

****

The black-and-white movie played across the screen as James snored on the love seat, his legs draped over Alex's lap. Alex's head was tipped back on the cushions, his eyes closed. Camille's family had left hours ago, and Mom and Dad were tucked in their bed upstairs. The twinkling tree was the only light in the room other than the soft glow of the dying fire.

Bea peeked at Aiden from the corner of her eye. He was awake on the other side of the couch. They shared a green-and-red plaid blanket, but their legs didn't touch. Not even by accident. Almost as if every time she shifted, he shifted too, away from her. Apparently, she had chosen the wrong cookies.

She wasn't crazy. Cookies didn't make people fall in love. Despite the fact she was young and blonde and female, and no one took her seriously, she wasn't stupid. She was getting a master's degree in biochemical engineering for Christ's sake. But at this point, anything to tip the scales in her favor was welcome. Plus, there was no such thing as too many cookies.

On screen, the hero kissed his wife and finally realized he was the richest man in town. His little curly-headed daughter rang the freaking bell, and tears rolled down Bea's cheeks. Every damn time. She sniffed and wiped her face with her hand.

Aiden turned. "You okay?" His voice was low, trying not to wake anyone.

"This movie. It gets to me. Are you not crying?"

He shook his head. "Movies don't make me cry."

What? She had studied this man for the past ten Christmases. How had she missed this? "How does this movie not make you cry? This movie makes everyone cry." She turned so they faced each other on the couch. Their knees almost touched. Aiden's mouth turned up in the corner.

"It just doesn't."

"That worries me."

He let out a small laugh. "Oh yeah?"

"Yes. I'm quite concerned," she teased. "Do you have a heart inside your chest or is it like a Tin Man situation?" She pressed her palm to his chest. Big mistake. His body was long and lean, and his chest was as firm as she imagined. She reluctantly pulled her hand away. Aiden watched her with his warm brown eyes. Was he closer than he was a minute ago?

"There's a heart in there, but sappy movies don't have much of an effect on it." He was definitely closer. Her knee pressed against his. Holy shit. Maybe the cookies had worked. Aiden's gaze was on her lips as he leaned toward her. He was so close now his breath whispered across her face. His gaze flicked up to hers. His pupils were rimmed in gold.

"So what does affect your heart?" Her voice was barely a whisper.

Aiden tucked an escaped curl behind her ear, and his fingers brushed her cheek. Her heart slammed into her rib cage. *Holy sweet baby Jesus, Aiden McLean is about to kiss me.*

Bea closed her eyes, her lips parted slightly, waiting.

"Is the movie over already?" James's voice tore through the room, and Aiden lunged to his side of the couch so fast Bea had whiplash.

Alex yawned dramatically from the love seat as he stretched his hands overhead. "I always miss the end. Is life still worth living or does he jump this time?"

Aiden's strangled laugh was too loud in the quiet room. James raised his eyebrow, a bemused smirk on his lips.

"Still worth it," Aiden choked out.

"Okay…" James dragged out the last syllable, glancing between her and Aiden, who looked like he just committed a murder. There was so much space between them he might as well have been in another room.

"Well, we're going to bed." Alex tugged James from his seat, giving Bea and Aiden a knowing smile. Her cheeks heated. Those two were about as subtle as a gay pride parade. Did he wink at her? She'd kill them both later.

"Goodnight," James practically sang as Alex dragged him from the room.

They were alone again in the soft glow of the fire. Aiden shifted next to her and cleared his throat. The movie credits scrolled across the screen, and Bea wished there was a way to rewind to the last scene, to when her hand was on Aiden's chest, and his eyes were on hers, and they were so close…

"Well." His voice cut through her thoughts.

"Want to watch something else?" She blurted it out before he had a chance to say anything. She turned to face him again, and his lips tipped into a smile. For a minute it seemed he would agree, like he might scoot closer to her again, stay up late with her, and watch another movie. Instead, he gave a small shake of his head, and the smile faded from his face.

"I need sleep."

"Sure. Of course." She nodded like this made perfect sense, like she wasn't disappointed. "I'll see you in the morning."

He tugged the blankets off and stood over her. He hesitated, looking like he might say more, but he shook his head again.

"Goodnight, Bea."

"Goodnight, Aiden." She watched him go before she flipped on the next movie.

Chapter Two

December 1965
Rose and Patrick, the Grandparents

The fire station was decked out in lights and holiday cheer. The band played Christmas classics on repeat, and couples spun lazily around the dance floor. A tribe of children roamed wild, armed with candy canes, and dressed in Santa hats. Rose scanned the room from her spot behind the refreshment table.

She had run the table for the ladies' auxiliary club for the past three years. Christmas cookies of every kind, shape, and flavor, along with holiday punch—the smell of which burned her nostrils—were laid out in front of her. People would be tipsy in no time.

There were others who could run the table, but she didn't have a date anyway. So here she was again, observing from behind the safety of the sweets.

When Patrick walked, no, not walked. Swaggered? Sauntered? Floated into the room—she was the first to notice. His dark hair was slicked to the side, and his blue eyes sparkled.

He headed straight for her table. She rearranged the plates again, lined up the napkins, restacked the cups, and when she looked up, he was in front of her. *Jesus, Mary, and Joseph pray for me.* He was more beautiful up close.

"Everything looks good. What do you recommend?"

His blue eyes gazed directly into hers, and she nearly fainted. He had never spoken to her before.

"Well…um…" *Speak Rose.* "I made these." She pushed the small plate of butter cookies toward him. He grabbed one and popped it into his perfect mouth.

"Delicious."

Her breath left her body in a shuttering exhale. She managed a smile. "Thanks."

"What's your name?"

"Rose."

"Pretty name."

Holy Lord, was Patrick flirting with her? A Christmas miracle indeed.

"So, Rose. Do you need to guard this table all night or are you allowed to dance?"

Dance? He wanted to dance? With her? *Breathe, Rose.*

"Um…I can…I mean I'm allowed to…"

"Perfect." He didn't wait for her to finish stuttering but took her hand and led the way to the dance floor, freeing her from the prison of baked goods. He pulled her close, and they rocked in a slow circle in time to the music. His chest was warm and firm under her cheek. It was official. She could die happy now.

They danced the whole night. Fast, slow, and impossibly close. He was a good dancer, moved easily to the music. She was a mess, but he didn't seem to mind. He didn't glance at another girl, although plenty stared at him.

When the band played the last song of the evening, Rose fought the urge to cry. The night had been perfect, but she didn't expect it to happen again. She wasn't that lucky.

"Can I get your phone number?" Patrick helped her with her coat as he asked. She slipped her arm in the sleeve and waited for him to grab a piece of paper, a napkin, a pen, anything.

"You're not going to write it down?"

He smiled. "I'll remember it."

Rose rattled off her parents' phone number, but her stomach ached in disappointment. The odds of him remembering it were slim to none.

"I had a nice night, Rose."

"Me too." Her voice was quiet in the night air. He walked her as far as the front of the fire station but didn't linger. He strode off to find his friends, leaving her to climb into the passenger seat of her father's car. She was silent on the drive home. It had all been a dream, and she dreaded tomorrow when her life returned to normal.

So, imagine her surprise when the phone rang the next day.

"Rose, phone for you," her sister called. "Someone named Patrick."

A Christmas miracle.

****

Christmas Day, Present Day

By the time Aiden woke up on Christmas morning, voices drifted down the hall to his bedroom along with the smell of freshly baked cookies. Did she make them for breakfast? He ran a hand down his face and scrubbed, rousing himself into action.

He wasn't eager to see Bea again after last night. He had gotten dangerously close to acting on his desires, the ones he had kept hidden for the past seven Christmases.

It wasn't his fault, though. He blamed that damn movie and its saccharine sweetness. After James and Alex went to bed, he had been so tempted to stay awake with her. For them to be alone together, for her to put her hand on his chest again. For so many things.

He closed his eyes and imagined the way she looked in the glow of the fire. Her plump lips asked to be kissed. Everything about her was soft and delicious. He groaned and rolled over. Now he had to wait for his cock to stand down before joining everyone for presents.

He needed to get a grip. Bea was off-limits. He repeated this mantra as he pushed her mouthwatering curves from his mind.

First of all, she was his best friend's sister. Wasn't there a rule about that somewhere? Second, despite the fact he had nothing but non-brotherly feelings for her, her family was his chosen family. Any normal person would think of her as practically a sibling, right? And third, there was the very real inevitability that he would fuck it up with her. And then what? Spending Christmas with his mom's second family in California, pretending everyone was cool with him being there was not his idea of a happy holiday. Not to mention, he hated the thought of Bea one day despising him for breaking her heart. He liked the possibility of her breaking his heart even less.

By the time he finished his list, his penis was as depressed as he was, but at least he was presentable for a wholesome family Christmas morning. He rolled out of bed and pulled on a gray sweater over his T-shirt but left his sweatpants on. The rest of the family dressed in their holiday jammies for Christmas morning, but that was where he drew the line. No sledding penguin loungewear for him.

"Aiden." James greeted him with a smile as soon as he emerged into the living room. James had always been a morning person. It was one of the few things Aiden hated about him.

"Morning," he managed as he shuffled into the kitchen for coffee. Bea was armed with a new plate of cookies. Chocolate balls dusted liberally with powdered sugar.

"Merry Christmas," she chirped, holding out the tray.

"Cookies for breakfast?" He looked at her, searching for any sign she was as affected by last night as he was. Maybe he had imagined the whole thing.

"Why not? It's Christmas." She wore an apron over her pajamas, and her hair was in a messy bun. A streak of flour ran across her cheek. She must have woken up at the crack of dawn to make this batch. His fingers twitched at his side with the urge to wipe the flour from her face.

"Oh, breakfast cookies. Yum." Alex came up behind him and grabbed a cookie from the tray. He grinned as he popped the confection into his mouth and nearly skipped over to the coffee maker. "Can I pour you a cup, Aiden?"

Aiden nodded. Bea chimed in with his order, saving him the labor of attempting speech before coffee. "He takes it with cream, no sugar." She still held the plate of cookies, so Aiden took one and shoved it into his mouth.

"Good, right?" She watched him eat it. What was going on with her? Was she in a cookie baking contest and he was her guinea pig?

"Mmhmm."

Alex handed him a mug, and he washed the cookie

down with the lifesaving liquid. His humanity slowly returned.

Pleased with his answer, Bea returned to the living room with her parents and brother, gathered around the tree in their matching PJs. They belonged in a brochure. Come vacation in New Hampshire. The perfect place for your holiday season!

His own family had never been picture-perfect. He hadn't seen his dad since he was a kid, and his mother remarried when he was in college. Her new family suited her better. None of them looked like the man who left her, which was a big part of their appeal.

She moved across the country to be with her new husband and his three children. Aiden heard from her once a month or so, but it never seemed worth it to travel to California for Christmas. That was how he ended up tagging along on James's Christmas vacations ten years ago. And he was still here.

Bea laughed at something her mother said, and James shoved her onto the couch, calling her a nerd. Aiden looked into his mug; the familiar feeling he didn't belong slid through him and settled into his stomach.

"Aren't we lucky?" Alex stood beside him, sipping his coffee and watching the antics in the living room.

"Um…lucky?"

"We get to join this family. Pretty lucky, if you ask me."

Aiden nearly choked on his coffee. "Well, you get to join this family. I show up here on the holidays like a stray pet." He hadn't meant for his voice to sound so bitter, but it did.

Alex peered at Aiden over his mug. He was shorter than him and James but solidly built. His face was covered in dark stubble, and he had on glasses instead of contacts this morning. He was different from James's past boyfriends, mainly because he wasn't an asshole. Aiden liked him already.

"You're more a part of this family than I am. James considers you a brother."

Aiden looked over to where Bea giggled on the couch as James did his best impression of her as a cookie-slinging Christmas maniac. He was a part of this family, and that was part of the problem.

"They look ready to open gifts." He left Alex standing at the counter, eyeing him suspiciously, and headed for the tree.

****

Bea slumped into the couch cushions, surrounded by torn wrapping paper, ribbons, and cookie crumbs. Her blood zipped through her veins, and she was slightly nauseous. Apparently, cookies and coffee for breakfast was not the best idea.

Scents of bacon and eggs wafted from the kitchen where her father had strapped on his Santa apron and was whipping up a proper breakfast.

Aiden sat on the far side of the room, laughing with James and Alex. How was it possible for him to act normal when all she could think about was their almost-kiss?

Aiden was never perky first thing in the morning. Past Christmases taught her that. But he was on his second cup of coffee and seemed normal. Happy, even. Had she imagined last night? Was it all the movie and the twinkly lights and the warm fire? A trick of ambiance and Christmas magic?

He glanced over at her, and she tore her gaze away,

pretending to be engrossed in her new book. Alex and James wandered off to the kitchen, and she almost rose to join them, but before she moved Aiden was next to her on the couch. She slammed the book shut, hoping he didn't get a look at the absolute smut she was reading.

"Merry Christmas." He placed a large square box in her lap. It looked like a child had wrapped it. She grinned.

"For me? I thought I opened all of mine."

Aiden ducked his head, running a hand over the back of his neck. "It's nothing much. Something I saw and thought you'd like it."

Bea's blood moved faster than before. She worried she might die of a heart attack before she got to see what was in this poorly wrapped package. She sat up straighter, took a deep breath, and ripped through the paper, revealing a pair of white ice skates.

"Aiden…" She ran a loving hand over the box, smiling so hard her cheeks ached. A faint blush crept up Aiden's face, filling her with almost as much joy as the gift itself.

"It's nothing." He shifted next to her. "Like I said, I saw the skates and…um…they reminded me of you."

It was not nothing. He had wrapped up her favorite memory and given it to her as a gift. Very different from last year's generic coffee shop gift card. Her family being in the open kitchen several feet away was the only thing keeping her from tackling him. Although they were so deep in mimosas at this point, she'd be surprised if they noticed.

"Did you bring yours?"

"Well, I can't send you out on the lake by yourself."

She stared at him, slack-jawed. Drool was seconds

away from dribbling down her chin. He remembered.

The first time they had skated together was seven Christmases ago. A memory she held absurdly close to her heart considering nothing happened. It was after her first semester of college, and she was homesick the whole time. Skating around the lake like they used to when she and James were kids was the one thing she asked for that year. But James was busy nursing a broken heart and had refused to do anything joyful.

Aiden had agreed to take her, and she spent the entire time pretending she was a horrible skater, falling all over him. She assumed he came with her to get away from her sad sack of a brother or because he was sorry for her. But the way he looked at her now, maybe she had been wrong.

"I love it." Her voice was barely a whisper. "Now I feel like an asshole for getting you a scarf."

He huffed a laugh, his eyes crinkling in the corners. God, he looked so good in that sweater, with his hair all mussed from sleep. A sexy and rumpled Aiden in her bed factored heavily into her Christmas morning fantasies. Her heart did a little sigh in her chest.

"It's a really nice scarf." His hand rested on her pajama-clad knee, right over a sledding penguin. When had it landed there? The warmth seeped through the fuzzy fabric and seared her skin. He must have realized it was there at the same time she did. He pulled his hand away and tucked it under his crossed arms, as though restraining himself.

Every fleecy penguin screamed in despair.

Plates clattered in the kitchen, and her father announced breakfast was ready. Aiden was gone, heading toward the food, and her knee was back to being sad and cold in the blink of an eye. Damn it.

Chapter Three

It was a horrible idea. That much was clear to him now. A fucking horrible idea.

Bea bounded out of the house, looking fucking adorable in her sweater and puffy vest. Her hair escaped the sides of her hat and curled around her face, and her cheeks were already pink in the cold. She looked perfect, and it might kill him.

The ice skates, the horrible idea ice skates, hung over her shoulder, the blades glinting in the sunlight.

"Ready?" she asked when she reached where he stood in the driveway, regretting his choices. "Want to walk? It's such a nice day."

"Sure." He yanked his old skates from the trunk of his car. His attempt at enthusiasm was strained even to his own ears.

Bea twisted her perfect lips. "If you don't want to come…"

"No. I mean, yes. I mean, I do want to come." *Very smooth.*

"Okay, because I'm sure Camille has a pair of skates somewhere. I can always go with her."

"No, I'm fine. I'm a little tired from all the celebrating, but the fresh air will revive me." He nearly grabbed her hand, forgetting everything he shouldn't do.

Can't have that. He shoved his hands into his pockets and strode into the woods toward the lake. Bea crunched along beside him in the snow.

It wasn't a lie. The fresh air helped. He woke up prickly and restless this morning, hot and sluggish from all the eating and celebrating. He sucked in the cold, piney air and cleared his head.

Unfortunately, once clear, the first thing that rushed in was the memory of the last time he took Bea ice-skating. He hadn't thought much about her before that year. She was his roommate's little sister, too young to be interesting. But that year he noticed her.

She was cute and funny, and her nose had this way of crinkling when she laughed that had him doing stupid shit all week. He wanted to be the reason she did those adorable things.

All she wanted that year was for James to take her skating, but the latest asshole to break up with him had him too focused on his own issues to see how much his sister needed this family moment.

So Aiden offered to take her, and her face lit up. He chased that feeling—the one he got when she looked at him—for years and never found it anywhere else.

They spent the whole afternoon skating around the frozen shoreline. Bea slipped and slid until he held her hand tight to keep her steady. He wanted to kiss her at the end of it, ask her out, tell her how he felt. Anything. But he balked.

That was the year his mother made it official and married his stepdad, the year James called him his brother, the year he adopted the Millers as his new family. So what was he going to do? Announce he planned to date one of them? *Not gonna happen.*

He tried to forget how Bea's hand fit so perfectly in his, and how her laugh was his favorite sound, and how she looked first thing Christmas morning. He only had to see her once a year. It was doable. Or that's what he told himself as he suffered through Christmas dinner after Christmas dinner, staring at Bea across the table. It was far safer than the alternative.

He glanced at her from the corner of his eye. God, she was so fucking beautiful. She caught him looking and grinned. And the day brightened.

"I brought cookies." She pulled a small bag from the pocket of her vest. "Want one?"

He held out a gloved hand, and she placed a cookie on it. He took a bite. It was a simple cookie this time, no sprinkles or frosting, chewy and familiar.

"Molasses?"

"Yep."

"Are you shooting for a new record this year?"

She giggled, and he snuck a peek at her crinkled nose. Damn, why was her nose so cute? How was a man supposed to ignore such a cute fucking nose?

She wiped the crumbs from her hands on the front of her jeans. "Nope. I'm in the mood for cookies. That's all."

He popped the rest of the cookie in his mouth. The sugar dissolved on his tongue, bringing with it the memories of every other Christmas spent with the people he loved. But this Christmas was different. Bea was chipping away at his resolve. Bea and her sunny smile, and her infectious laugh, and all her damn cookies. His reasons for staying away from her slipped from his grasp. And maybe he wanted to let them go.

Aiden let out a sigh, the sound too loud in the quiet

woods. Bea sent him a questioning look, but he forced a smile and sat on a fallen log to lace up his skates.

The lake stretched out ahead of them, its cold gray surface dotted with red ice fishing tents. Aiden's lungs burned as he sucked in the icy air. He focused on his frozen fingertips as he tied his skates instead of Bea's warm body next to him. They were alone in their own little cove surrounded by towering pines. It would be easy to forget why he shouldn't hold her hand, or pull her close, or cover her lips with his. And he couldn't let that happen.

Why had he brought her here? Why torture himself like this? He didn't have an answer. He saw the skates and wanted nothing more than to bring her here again. He wrapped them quickly, packing his feelings up along with the skates, refusing to think about what he was doing. But now the box was open, and here he was in the spot where he fell in love with her, pretending he wasn't in love with her. A fucking horrible idea.

"Ready?" Bea stood and brushed the snow from her ass.

Aiden squeezed his eyes shut, blocking out the image of her hands moving over her ample curves. Thinking about Bea's ass was the last thing he needed. "Ready as I'll ever be," he muttered, standing to join her. They teetered toward the ice, their skates crunching in the crusty snow. Bea's hand hung next to his, but she didn't reach for him. Disappointment spiked through him.

She stepped onto the ice, slid gracefully across the bumpy surface, did a little spin, and turned to face him.

His mouth dropped open. "What the hell was that?" He shoved his hands into his coat pockets.

"What do you mean?" Her eyes were wide with feigned innocence.

He skated to where she'd stopped, a spot of color in the midst of all the gray. "You're a terrible skater."

"Oh, yeah. I'm actually not." She grinned.

"Yes, you are. The last time we did this you fell all over the place." He was dangerously close to her now. Her vanilla scent overtook the smell of the pines. She tipped her face up to his.

"Maybe it was an excuse to hold your hand."

He blinked and she skated off, her laugh floating back to him as she went. He skated after her, getting his footing. His years of peewee hockey were finally paying off. Blades scraped the ice as he outpaced her. He made an abrupt stop, spraying ice on her new skates, and turned to look at her.

"You were pretending?" His cheeks burned with the cold and something else. Embarrassment? Disappointment? Whether he wanted to admit it or not, he brought her here to hold her hand. And now he didn't get to. *Pitiful.*

Her eyes were full of mischief, and her lips were so damn pink and kissable he might die right here on the ice from wanting her.

"You knew I had a crush on you."

"I didn't know," he lied. Of course, he did, but he liked hearing her say it. It was like pushing on a bruise to see if it still hurt.

"You didn't know? I always assumed you did." She pushed at his chest, and he coasted backward.

"I guess I wasn't paying attention." Another lie. He always paid attention to her.

"I guess not." She skated past him, making lazy

circles around their section of the lake. He watched her, his toes going numb inside his skates. Was it too late to pretend he forgot how to skate? Would she hold his hand if he did? A fucking horrible idea.

****

Aiden stood frozen where she left him. Was he that oblivious? She was not subtle, especially as a teenager. She always assumed he saw right through her flimsy excuses to spend time with him. Even if he didn't realize she still harbored feelings for him now, they must have been obvious then. Right?

She pined after him for ten years, and he hadn't had a freaking clue. The man was maddening. But no matter. This was the year she changed everything. Maybe molasses cookies were the cookies. He seemed to like them best so far, anyway.

He shook his head, waking from his stupor, and skated toward her. Bea sped up. Aiden skated faster. Let him chase her for a change. She surged forward, the cold wind stinging her cheeks. Her lungs filled with icy air and blew out puffs of steam. It was good to be outside. Cozy was only cozy for so long. After a while it became stuffy.

Her toe hit a bump in the ice and she careened forward, bracing herself for the fast-approaching ground. But she never hit it. Aiden wrapped his arm around her waist, holding her up. He pulled her in close, and they both slipped and slid. For a second it seemed they might fall, but they found their balance. When she turned to face him, they were toe to toe. Their breath fogged the air and mingled between them.

"Thanks."

"You got cocky there, little Miss 'I'm Actually A

Great Skater.' "

"Yeah well…" Any snappy retort she might have had left her brain as soon as she looked up and found him staring at her. Her hands still lay on his chest, and his heart raced beneath his sweater. He gripped her hips and held her in place. The two inches of space between them could be easily breached by a small slide of an ice skate.

"So." He cleared his throat. "Tell me more about this crush." His mouth lifted in a half-smile, and Bea wanted nothing more than to kiss the smirk off his face.

"It was a silly crush." Her voice was husky. His fingers tightened on her hip bones.

He raised an eyebrow. "Oh?"

"Typical teenage girl stuff. Older brother brings home a hot roommate. You know how it goes." She tried to be flippant, but his eyes hadn't left hers. They widened when she said, "Hot roommate."

"Hot, huh?"

She licked her bottom lip, and Aiden's gaze followed her tongue across her mouth. He slid her closer. The nearness of his body warmed her, in more ways than one.

"Hot might have been James's word," she said, teasing him. But at the mention of James, Aiden slid back and dropped his hands from her hips, like he had suddenly remembered he was allergic to her. Cold air rushed into the space he had filled. Damn it. Why had she brought up her brother at a time like this?

Aiden lowered his gaze, studying his skates.

"He has good taste, though." She tried to salvage the moment, but it was too late.

He gave a small laugh and took off again, Bea gliding by his side.

"Anyway, I figured you didn't see me as anything other than James's sister so…"

"So?" He glanced at her out of the corner of his eye. Now was the time for honesty. Now was the time to tell him she wanted to be with him. But Bea wasn't in the habit of proclaiming her true feelings. She was a people pleaser, agreeable to a fault. People liked her for a reason.

She swallowed hard. If she believed Aiden wanted to hear she was still in love with him and had been since she was fifteen, she would have told him. But he had gone all stiff and cold, increasing the distance between them more and more. His body language said, stay away. So she agreed with him. It was what she did.

"So, I had to let it go."

"Oh." The sound was small and…sad? He cleared his throat again. "I'm glad you didn't waste too much time on me." His smile was strained.

Shit. Had she misread him? Did he want her to say she still had a crush on him? Did he have a crush on her? Her mind was a swirl of teenage angst she thought she had left behind years ago and with it the familiar panic of not knowing what to say or do.

"Let's head back," he said. "I'm freezing."

"Of course." She pulled the cookies from her pocket and stuffed two more in her mouth. The molasses turned bitter on her tongue as she followed Aiden off the ice.

Chapter Four

December 1990
Fran and Cole, the Parents

"You going to finish that?" She didn't give him a chance to say no. She was already eating the last of the baked ziti from his plate as she slipped into the seat across from him. Fran didn't know anyone at this party. Her best friend Marian had dragged her here, and now, said best friend was nowhere to be found.

"I guess not," the handsome stranger said as she slid his plate to her side of the table. The trays of food in the kitchen were scraped clean, and she was starving.

"I'm Fran." She introduced herself between bites of his dinner.

"Cole." He leaned back in his chair, arms across his chest, watching her with a bemused smile. His hair was golden even in the dim light of the party, and he looked like he belonged on a sailboat or in an L.L.Bean catalog. And despite the fact there was a foot of snow outside, Fran wouldn't be surprised if she looked under the table and found he was wearing boat shoes. His hideous Christmas sweater and lopsided smile softened his perfections and turned him into a real human boy. One she'd like to get to know, or at least spend more time looking at.

"Well, Cole, I can't stand to see pasta go to waste."

She grinned at him as she twirled his fork between her fingers.

He watched her as she polished off the rest of his food, legs stretched out, arms still crossed like he was relaxing at the helm of his boat. Fran imagined the sea air ruffling his blond hair, an image so out of place in this tiny apartment in Charlestown, she nearly laughed.

A string of Christmas lights, the big kind that got hot to the touch, hung over their heads, and music blared from a nearby boombox.

She leaned across the table so he could hear her better. "So did you get dragged here too?"

He laughed a little and shook his head. "It's my cousin's party." He broke his leisurely pose to lean in, too. Their faces were close enough now to see the golden tips of his eyelashes. "I made the ziti by the way. Glad you liked it so much."

She quirked an eyebrow. Now, this was something. A pretty, preppy boy who made good Italian food. Impossible to resist. She stretched, reaching toward the coffee table—without leaving her seat, thanks to the tininess of the space—and grabbed a plate of cookies.

"I made these." She held out the plate of butter cookies glittering with colored sugar. He took one, popped the whole thing in his mouth, and immediately took another. She smiled.

He glanced around the party, taking in the empty red cups, the half-drunk guests, and the sad silver Christmas tree in the corner. "Do you want to get out of here?" he asked, swiping another cookie for the road.

"Definitely."

They burst out into the cold night air, arms linked, and headed for the nearest coffee shop. By the next morning, Fran had discovered Cole had never been on a sailboat, but loved the beach, had finished culinary school but ate primarily bacon and eggs, and his laugh was so big and loud it attracted the attention of everyone within a fifty-foot radius. And also, she was in love with him.

Call it luck or Christmas miracles, he loved her too. They were married six months later.

****

December 27, Present Day

"You know Christmas is over, right?" Aiden sat next to her on the couch, where she was curled up watching sappy holiday movies. His appearance made her realize she hadn't moved from her blanket-filled nest for hours.

She hadn't seen Aiden all day. They all learned years ago the key to a successful family week of togetherness was strategic time apart. Even still, she was certain he had been avoiding her since their awkward ice-skating trip. Something had been different, the way he looked at her, his hands on her hips. Something had shifted between them, but it slipped through her fingers before she could catch it.

Today, she had gone into town to shop after-Christmas sales with her mother and Camille, and Alex, Aiden, and James had gone skiing. She was pretty sure her father had read the newspaper for eight hours, which was his idea of the perfect day.

"And you are well aware in this family, Christmas isn't over until New Year's Day. So...shut up." She stuck her tongue out at him. The perfect way to remind him she was a grown-up.

He smirked, tugged one of the blankets away from her, and crawled under.

"How was skiing?" She tried to keep her voice light, but the promise of him next to her scrambled her thoughts.

"Not bad. James nearly killed himself on the black diamond, but it was entertaining for the rest of us."

She snuggled deeper under the blankets, and Aiden's warmth seeped into the space between them. She inched closer, and he didn't pull away. Their knees touched. Their arms met. She tipped her head and leaned it on his shoulder, each move a slow advance toward what she wanted. His body remained rigid for a breath, and then two, until he melted into her. Her nerve endings fizzed like she had Pop Rocks in her veins. Aiden this close was exhilarating.

"So, what's this one about? Besides Christmas magic and all that." His voice was low and teasing.

"Oh, you love it." She nudged his arm with her own, grateful for the break in the tension building inside her. He huffed grumpily but didn't protest.

"This is one of my favorites. The owner of the small-town bakery has been in love with her brother's friend for years." Her heart sped up as though her words were a confession, as though the movie was about her. It might as well have been.

"Oh yeah?"

"Yeah. But he's a big-city lawyer she sees once a year."

"Huh." He sank deeper into the couch cushions, and Bea snuggled into his side.

"Right. So he comes home and she, of course, shows him the meaning of Christmas."

"Naturally." She could hear the smile in his voice.

"And he realizes he's in love with her too."

He cleared his throat. "Of course."

His answer hung between them. Of course. Why couldn't it be simple? They sat in silence, watching the small-town girl charm the big-city guy. As expected, they knocked each other over during a snowball fight, decorated the enormous tree, and baked several hundred cookies together.

"The classic flour-on-the-cheek move," she murmured when the big-city guy wiped the flour from the girl's cheek, lingering too close, their lips nearly touching. Her favorite part.

"I have never once wiped baking ingredients from a woman's face."

"It must be why you're still single," she teased. "Clearly, you are doing it wrong."

"Clearly." They were so close, his answer whispered across her temple.

"I don't find that to be the most unrealistic part, though." She swallowed hard. This conversation was the closest she had ever come to admitting her feelings for him. The room, the cozy fire, the blankets, everything was suddenly too warm.

"Oh, no? Is it the inhuman amount of Christmas decor?" He gestured toward the movie and its over-the-top holiday aesthetic. "Or the fresh layer of snow around for the entire month of December?" Ice rain pelted the windows of their cabin, illustrating his point.

"Nope." Deep breath. "It's the fact they don't kiss until the end." They still faced the screen, but Aiden shifted next to her. "I mean, they obviously want to kiss each other right now. So why don't they?" Her words tumbled out in a rush before she could think better of it. She swallowed hard. Her mouth was suddenly dry.

"It's not always that simple." His answer was quiet, hesitant.

Bea lifted her head to face him. His gaze raked across her lips before returning to her eyes. Her heart raced in her chest, making her dizzy. She had never been this bold before, but this was Aiden. Her Aiden.

"Maybe it should be."

She leaned in, and he met her halfway. His nose brushed along her cheek. She sucked in a breath, flicking her gaze to his, warm brown with flecks of gold. He shifted toward her, studying her for a moment longer before making his decision. When his lips met hers, every atom in her body came alive. Every single one buzzed around and knocked into each other in a frenzy of excitement.

She put her hands on the sides of his face. His stubble was rough under her palms. He made a low hum of happiness on her lips. She smiled against his mouth. She ran her hands through his hair, and he kissed her deeper.

Holy Mother of Mary. Aiden McLean is kissing me. And it is amazing.

He pulled her closer, and she was suddenly acutely aware she was wearing sweats and an oversized sweater with no bra underneath. His hands wandered over her waist and down to her hips. Her lack of undergarments was about to make itself abundantly clear.

He kissed down her neck, and she moaned. And his hands, Christ, his hands were everywhere. He ran them across her stomach and up her back. When they ran over nothing but skin, he groaned into her mouth.

"Shit, Bea."

He pulled away from her lips, and she kissed

hungrily down his neck, nipping at his ears on her way. He smelled like the woods, pine, and the metallic tang of cold air. She inhaled him.

"Bea, wait." He grabbed her arms and held her away from him. Her lips stung from his stubble, and her cheeks were warm with desire.

"What's the matter?"

"I don't...I mean, we can't..." Three creases appeared between his brows, his worried face.

She blinked. Her cheeks went from delightfully warm to hot with embarrassment.

"Why not?"

"Because you're...I mean, your family...and me and your brother...and I can't..." His voice cracked.

She waited for more, an explanation for why they needed to stop when everything in her body shouted at her to go. But he stared at her, eyebrows furrowed, lips swollen from kissing her.

"Aiden, what are you talking about?"

"We need to stop. I'm too close to your family. You're like a sister to me." The words came out in a rush, strung together so tight Bea almost didn't understand. Almost.

Sister? The word was like a snowball to the face, unexpected and painful. After the initial shock, before she caught her breath, the icy misery of his words slid down her neck and seeped into the rest of her body. Sister. Was he kidding? One look at Aiden's face, his eyes squeezed shut like he couldn't bear to look at her, told her no, he wasn't kidding.

Bea nearly fell off the couch as she scrambled to put more space between them. "Your sister? I'm like a sister to you? Was that something you do with a sister?" Her voice got higher and louder with every question until she hit an octave that had the neighborhood dogs howling. She was hot and cold at once. The anger and embarrassment swirled together in her stomach.

Aiden hung his head in his hands. "No, I didn't mean it like that. I meant I'm so close to your family. I don't want to mess this up."

He looked at her, his face contorted as though this conversation caused him physical pain. He ran a hand roughly through his hair, leaving half of it standing up. The tortured look on his face was almost enough to soften her heart. But she was too pissed for sympathy.

The best kiss she had in her life, but he didn't feel the same.

Un-fucking-believable. Maybe he was right. Maybe it wasn't that simple.

"I'm going to bed." She was too embarrassed to listen to any more reasons why it was so abhorrent for him to kiss her.

"Bea, wait." His voice was strained.

"Forget it ever happened."

"Bea, come on. Let me explain better…"

"Goodnight."

He grabbed her hand as she turned to walk away. She stopped but didn't turn around. His jagged sigh pierced her heart but didn't undo his words.

"Goodnight," he said, still holding onto her hand. If she stayed, maybe this night could be salvaged, but self-preservation kept her turned away from him. She extracted her fingers from his and walked out of the living room, leaving the movie playing the happy ending and a plate full of uneaten thumbprint cookies sitting on the coffee table.

****

December 28, Present Day

Aiden knocked softly on James's door. He had replayed the kiss and its aftermath over in his head all night and had come to zero conclusions. Except that he was an idiot. That much was obvious.

"Come in."

Aiden opened the door into a scene of domestic bliss that did nothing to help his current mood. James sat on the bed, socked feet crossed at the ankles, computer on his lap. Alex was cozied up next to him, reading his latest romance novel. They both looked up when he walked in the door and closed it behind him.

"I fucked up." He blurted it out as soon as he was in the room.

"Okay…" James set aside his computer, and Alex stuck a bookmark on his page. "What did you do?"

Aiden leaned against the door and slid his fingers through his hair, which reminded him of Bea running her hands through it, which made him ache.

"I made out with your sister." He cringed, waiting for his friend's reaction.

James gasped in mock horror and then turned to Aiden in complete seriousness. "Finally."

"Finally?" Aiden's head snapped up and his gaze landed on James's amused face. "Aren't you supposed to be mad or something? Aren't you supposed to threaten me or warn me never to hurt your baby sister?"

James shrugged. "She's a big girl. You might have noticed."

Aiden groaned. He had noticed. That was the problem. "Well, I fucked it up so it doesn't matter now anyway."

"What happened?" Alex sat cross-legged, giving Aiden his undivided attention.

"I might have said she was like a sister to me. While we made out." He winced at the memory. It was by far one of the dumbest things he had ever said, not to mention the biggest lie. But he had panicked. He said the first thing that came to mind in an attempt to slow things down between them. Or bring them to a screeching halt.

James laughed and leaned his head against the headboard. "Jesus, Aiden."

"I know." He groaned again and scrubbed a hand down his heavily stubbled jaw. He needed to shave, but apparently blowing up his life took precedence today.

"I haven't kissed a lot of women, but even I know that's wrong." Alex laughed but reined it in when he saw Aiden slumped against the door.

He hadn't meant to hurt her. He wanted to stop before he did something they'd both regret.

"Did you come in here hoping I would forbid you from seeing her? Are you looking for an excuse to not try again?"

Was he that transparent? That was exactly what he wanted James to do. Bea would never want him to jeopardize his friendship with her brother. Preserving his relationship with James was the perfect out.

"I'm not going to do it. In fact, I think you two are good together." He folded his hands in his lap, the declaration made.

"I'm sure she'll forgive you. Show her you don't see her that way." Of course, Alex's suggestion was entirely reasonable, but Aiden wasn't feeling particularly reasonable today. Or anytime he was around Bea.

Aiden shook his head. "I need her to forgive me. But

that's it."

"What do you mean?"

"I mean if I date Bea and we break up, I lose her and I lose you. And I lose this…" He gestured around the room, the cabin, the whole Christmas experience. If he screwed it up with Bea, the few people he cared to call family disappeared from his life.

"You won't lose me. Don't be so melodramatic." James scooted to the edge of the bed and dangled his legs over the side, studying his friend.

"It would change everything," Aiden argued.

"And your life is so perfect now you don't want to change it? You enjoy pining over my sister every year?" James countered, eyebrows raised.

"I…how did you…" How was everyone better in tune with his emotions than he was?

"I'm not blind. Or stupid."

"Go for it." Alex smiled at him with all the confidence of a man who had already found the love of his life and locked it down.

"I second that. Now go convince my sister you have nothing but non-brotherly affection for her."

"Good luck," Alex called as Aiden closed the door behind him.

****

He found Bea in the kitchen, furiously mixing something in an oversized bowl. Her back was to him, and he slouched in the doorway watching her work. Her hair was piled on top of her head like it usually was when she cooked. A few curls had escaped and brushed the nape of her neck. He envied those curls. The memory of the softness of her skin and the heat of her lips was still fresh in his mind.

Melissa McTernan

The words he needed to speak stuck in his throat like his body rejected the idea of saying them. He cleared his throat, and she turned, her blue eyes widening in surprise at finding him there. And the inevitability of their ending flashed through his mind. It was easy to imagine those blue eyes filled with tears because of him.

Which was why it was better to never start something than to have it end. It didn't matter what James said. Sating his deep-seated desire for her was not worth the risk of hurting her.

"You scared me," she said, her voice hard, all her usual cheer gone. She put the bowl down and scooped the cookie dough onto an empty tray.

"Sorry." He had a lot more to apologize for than scaring her. "I'm sorry about last night, too."

Color seeped into her cheeks, but she didn't take her gaze off the baking tray. No one had ever put more focus into a batch of cookies than she was now.

"Let's forget about it." She banged the spoon on the edge of the tray, dislodging the cookie dough. The harsh sound punctuated her answer.

Right. Forget about it. That's exactly what he needed to do, but he had embarrassed and confused her. He had to fix that first.

"I can't forget about it."

Her gaze shot to his, full of unanswered questions and the tiniest flicker of hope. It was the hope that did him in. He was fucking this up eight different ways but was unable to stop himself.

"I didn't mean it, about you being like a sister to me." He swallowed, took a breath. "It's not true."

He didn't remember stepping toward her, but suddenly he was right in front of her, too close. He came in here to tell her their first kiss had to be their last, and now he was dangerously close to leaning down and covering her lips with his. What was wrong with him?

"Oh?" Her question was all innocence, but her gaze dragged over his mouth.

He cleared his throat. "But it can't happen again." Bea took a step back as though his words had sharp edges and she was afraid of getting cut. He needed to say everything this time, needed her to understand.

"I should think of you like a sister. Your family…they mean a lot to me. I don't want to make things weird."

"Weird?"

Damn it. Why was this so hard? Tell her you can't be anything more than friends and get the hell out of the kitchen.

"We're friends. Let's stay friends." The word sounded wrong. He had never once thought of Bea as a friend. It was a wildly inadequate description of what she was to him, but it was all he had.

"You want us to be friends?" The incredulous look she gave him said he might as well have told her he wanted them to be a gangsta rap duo.

"Yeah. Friends." That word, that stupid, inaccurate word nearly choked him.

Bea nodded slowly, processing this information. There was a streak of flour on her cheek. That's when he made a fatal error. He cupped Bea's face in his hand and brushed it off with his thumb, her soft skin beneath his fingers.

She looked at him and her eyes filled with hope again. She smiled.

"Okay, we can be friends."

He yanked his hand away and fled the kitchen before he made any more mistakes.

Chapter Five

Last December
James and Alex, the Brother

"The cookies have arrived." James swept into the break room with a tray of butter cookies balanced on his hand. There was only one person here deserving of these magic cookies, but it seemed rude to point that out. So, he brought enough for everyone.

Alex peered at him over the rim of his coffee mug, amused. Maybe? James got the impression he didn't like him. Or maybe Alex wasn't as impressed with him as he wanted him to be. It was fine, though. He had the cookies now.

He laid the plate with a flourish on the break room table.

"Thanks, James! These look delicious."

He smiled at Linda, or Lucy, or whatever her name was from accounting. The cookies were not about her, but she was welcome to have some. He nudged the plate closer to Alex.

"What are your plans for Christmas?" Lulu or Lilly or what's her face asked him. He had to tear his gaze away from Alex to answer.

"Oh, my family and I go to our cabin in New Hampshire every year."

"How nice," the accounting lady cooed.

James nodded, turning to Alex. His plan was to use this opportunity to impress him. Alex had been working at the firm for a few months, but James spotted him immediately. He was sweet and funny, and his ass, dear God, perfection.

Unfortunately, his cookie plan was backfiring. The table now swarmed with hungry coworkers all chatting away about holiday plans and making it impossible for James to get a word in edgewise.

"Did you say, New Hampshire?" Harold from marketing boomed next to him and by the time he finished answering fifty questions about the best places to ski, eat, and shop in New Hampshire, Alex had returned to his cubicle. Damn it. Harold could Google it next time.

James swiped the last two cookies from the tray before the vultures had a chance to finish them off. He wrapped them in a napkin and moseyed over to Alex's desk. Leaning on the side of his cubicle, James strove for casual. He wasn't sure it came off.

"I brought you a couple of cookies. I didn't know if you got any. These people are animals."

Alex smiled.

James's heart fluttered. His heart did not typically flutter because of a pretty face. Hence the cookies. Alex took the napkin and nibbled a cookie.

"Mmm. Yummy." He hadn't taken his gaze off James since he arrived with his sugary offering. He ate the rest of the cookie and started on the other.

"How about we grab drinks later?" James had to act fast, while the magic of the cookies was working. Alex grinned, finished off the last of the cookies, and licked his fingers.

"I'd love to."

When James asked Alex to marry him nearly a year later, he said the same.

****

December 29, Present Day

"This might sound crazy, but have you tried telling him the truth?" Camille sipped her margarita and grabbed another chip. They were the first to arrive at El Loco Mexican, the restaurant Bea chose to celebrate her birthday for the past five years. Nothing said congratulations on surviving another year of life like tacos and margaritas. And extra guacamole.

Bea shoveled the creamy green goodness into her mouth to avoid answering Camille's question. Her best friend raised a perfect black eyebrow, waiting for her response.

"Ugh. No. But what more was there to say? We were kissing, and it was amazing, and I'm sure he thought so too, and then he told me I'm like a sister to him." She slumped lower into her chair. Camille studied her.

"I still think you should tell him."

Bea groaned. "Yesterday, he claimed we should be friends. Friends! Like what the hell is that about?"

Camille's face crinkled in disgust at the word. "Friends? Yikes."

"Exactly." He hadn't meant it, though. She remembered how he looked when he said it like it hurt him as much as it hurt her. And when he brushed the flour from her cheek, he made every holiday movie fantasy she ever had come true. Nothing about the way he looked at her at that moment said, let's be friends. A small shiver ran through her at the memory.

Camille took another chip, her brow furrowed. "He

loves your family, Bea," she said at last. "Maybe he's nervous about you two being together. It's not crazy. If you guys break up, things get messy."

Bea opened her mouth ready to protest, but Aiden, Alex, and James arrived, followed by her parents. James practically shoved Aiden into the chair next to her, and he looked nearly as miserable as she felt.

"Happy Birthday," Alex chirped, sliding into the seat next to Camille, James on his other side. Her parents took the seats at the end.

As everyone shucked off coats and scarves and wished her a happy birthday as though they hadn't all told her this morning, Bea sipped her drink and considered what Camille had said. Maybe Aiden was nervous about things progressing between them. Maybe she had to show him how good things could be.

She slid closer to him. His gaze met hers when her leg brushed against his and she left it there.

"You done being mad at me?" he whispered while everyone got settled.

She nodded.

"Happy birthday, Bea." His voice caressed her ear like a promise of touches to come. His hand slid gently up her leg, and he kept it on her thigh, burning through her jeans. Not brotherly at all.

Bea limited her birthday meal to one margarita and two tacos. She had plans for her evening and she did not need drunkenness or stomach aches to stand in her way. It was her birthday, and she intended to get what she wanted. If after tonight, Aiden insisted there was nothing between them, she would let it go.

By the time the servers and her family sang an off-key rendition of "Happy Birthday" over a candle-lit churro, Bea was ready to go. She smiled politely, but Aiden moved his hand in languid circles over her thigh, and her vision blurred. She looked over at him as she blew out her candle, and he stared at her like he'd prefer to have her for dessert. She swallowed hard.

Fortunately for her, everyone was too full to eat much more, so a few bites of churro for appearances, and her father paid the bill. Aiden hadn't had anything to drink besides iced tea, so he poured Alex and James into the back seat of his car. They giggled together like teenagers.

Bea dropped off a tipsy Camille and raced to the cabin. Aiden was in the kitchen snacking on the snowman cookies she had made that afternoon when she opened the door. He leaned against the counter, but the lines of his body were anything but relaxed.

"Hey." He stopped mid-bite and raised his gaze to hers. The heat from the restaurant was still there.

"Where is everyone else?" she asked, peeling off her coat and boots.

"They went to bed." His voice was a throaty whisper in the quiet room.

Bea nodded, walking toward him, her heart racing. It was now or never. She stood in front of him so close she had to tip her face up to look at him.

He ran his thumb along her cheek, mimicking the lines he traced the day before, except this time there was no flour. This time he had no excuse for touching her. She stepped closer, and he dropped his forehead to hers with a soft groan. She skated her hands across his chest.

"What are we doing?"

"Being friendly, I guess." She had meant it as a joke, but he winced. Bea rushed to fill in the silence.

"It's one night, Aiden. That's all it has to be."

His gaze flicked to hers, searching. "One night," he repeated, his voice rough.

She nodded, and the tension left his body. One night to prove to him they belonged together. Or one night to get him out of her system for good. Either way, she planned to enjoy it.

She wrapped her arms around his neck and pulled him closer. When her lips met his, her whole body ignited. She kissed him deeper, running her hands through the back of his hair and down his neck, across his broad shoulders.

His hands gripped her hips and turned them both so her back was toward the island counter. He lifted her onto the surface and stood between her legs. She wrapped them around his back, trapping him and pulling him closer to her. He grinned onto her lips.

They kissed until Bea's lips and face and neck burned from Aiden's still unshaved face. She hadn't kissed like this in so long. It was delicious and torturous, and she wanted so much more. Aching, she put her hands on his chest and pulled away long enough to whisper, "Come to my room."

He stilled, and she held her breath. Another rejection would kill her. But he couldn't keep his gaze from her swollen lips. He tightened his arms around her and lifted her off the counter, his hands firmly gripping her ass. She kissed his neck as he carried her down the hall to her bedroom. They ricocheted off the walls, groping and kissing each other as they went. He nearly dropped her as he opened the door. Nervous giggles escaped her.

"Sorry." He sighed the word into her ear as he pushed the door open. He put her down gently once they were inside, and she closed the door behind them.

"Are you sure you want to do this?" The crease between his eyebrows deepened.

"Yes." She pushed him onto the bed and followed him. She was more sure about this than anything in her life, and she wasn't going to let him overthink it this time. So he was close with her family? Wasn't that a good thing?

She straddled him, pulling off his sweater and T-shirt, unwrapping her gift. He laughed a little as she tugged the shirts over his head. His body was long and lean and sprinkled with tattoos. She had seen the ones on his arms before, but she took her time examining the others as he lay spread out beneath her. She liked the view.

He squirmed a little as she ran her fingers over his chest and arms.

"Ticklish?" she asked, kissing along his ribs. He laughed and rolled over, taking her with him. But a tattoo next to his ribs caught her eye. It was a small bee, flying dangerously close to his heart. She ran a finger over it and he stilled.

"Aiden?"

"Yeah?" His voice was husky.

"You have a bee tattooed on your chest."

"Yes." One word like a breath out.

More questions about this little bee bubbled up inside her. Surely this bee so close to his heart held some significance. But he had gone tense as soon as she mentioned it, and she wasn't about to ruin this moment.

"I like it." She kissed him, and he relaxed under her touch. Her sweater quickly joined his on the floor and the heat of his skin against hers was enough to make her whimper. More. She wanted more. He yanked off her pants and admired her matching bra and panties for a few seconds before discarding them as well.

When she was naked, he pulled away, leaving her quivering on the bed. She sat up, clutching at the covers.

"Don't."

She met his gaze. He kneeled on the bed next to her. "I want to see you."

If it were possible to blush everywhere, she did. His gaze raked over her.

"Well, fair is fair," she whispered when the heat of his gaze threatened to singe her skin. She moved closer and tugged at his belt buckle. He stood, letting her undo his pants and slide them over his narrow hips. Hooking her fingers on the waist of his boxer briefs, she slid those down too.

Praise Jesus. Aiden McLean was naked in front of her, and he was every bit as perfect as she imagined. She bit her lower lip, and he grabbed her hips and pulled her closer until she kneeled on the edge of the bed.

He skimmed his hands over her skin, leaving a trail of goose bumps in their wake.

"So fucking beautiful." His voice was nothing but a sexy growl in her ear, and she lost all control. She grabbed his shoulders and pulled him on top of her, needing the weight of him pressing her into the mattress. The muscles of his back were taut beneath her fingers as she caressed his shoulders, his waist, and the delicious curve of his ass. He leaned on his elbows and ran his nose gently down the side of her face, his soft touch tickling her cheek.

"You're sure?" he asked again. Was it possible to make it more obvious? She was writhing naked beneath him, a handful of his ass in her palm and her mouth on his neck, but she told him again, she was sure.

"Don't overthink it." Her body molded to his. Didn't he see how well they fit? The bee on his skin vibrated with his heartbeat and so did she. Finally, he tore his gaze away from her face. He kissed a line down her neck and made her squirm. He lifted himself away from her body, and she tried to pull him down, her fingers digging into his shoulders.

"Where are you going?" Her voice was nearly a whine.

"I'm taking a little tour." He hovered over her and kissed his way across her collar bone, her chest, her breasts. He stopped for a detour there, kissing and licking and sucking until Bea's entire world was distilled down to the exquisite feeling of his mouth on her body.

When she was out of her mind with wanting, he left her breasts to rain kisses on her soft belly and sides. In other sexual situations, men were not given the chance to spend so much time near her stomach, but no man had ever made his desire for her so clear. It was intoxicating.

By the time Aiden settled at his destination between her legs, Bea was a hot bundle of raw nerve endings. When he finally licked between her thighs, they both moaned.

"Bea, you're sweet everywhere." His voice was filled with such reverent awe she wasn't embarrassed by his observation. Her legs fell open wider, and he grabbed her ass with both hands and continued tasting her. His tongue was a revelation.

It didn't take long before Bea fell apart under his touch. She plummeted over the edge, cramming a pillow over her face to muffle her screams. Her toes curled. Her whole body curled. Her leg twitched. Never in her life…

He crawled up her body and kissed her, her own sweetness still on his lips.

"Jesus Christ," she whispered.

He grinned.

A shyness crept over her, making her bury her face in the curve between his neck and shoulder when he lay beside her. *Aiden McLean watched her come. Sweet Lord.*

"We don't have to do anything else tonight." He spoke into the top of her head, his lips brushing against her hair.

Would there be other nights? More nights like this? She didn't dare ask. But more nights or not, she wasn't going to leave the man hanging. Well, not so much hanging as pointing straight up at the ceiling.

"No…I'm…fine."

"Fine?" He raised an eyebrow.

"Not fine," she corrected. "Amazing. Really, really amazing."

He let out a small laugh. "Bea, we can stop. I'll be okay."

She emerged from her hiding place and faced him. He rolled onto his side to look at her.

"I can't believe it's happening. It's you. And me."

He nodded, his stubble rasping against the pillow. Aiden, in her bed, looking like he belonged there. She rushed to fill in the silence.

"But it's good, right? I mean, are you having a good time?" She winced. What was she doing? Taking a survey in the middle of sex?

This time he laughed big and throaty, and his eyes crinkled adorably. "I'm having an incredible time." He ran a hand along her hip and over the curve of her butt and back again like a skier going downhill.

"Me too." Her voice was hoarse from panting. She inched closer and found the reassuring evidence he still wanted her pressed into her stomach. "It's your turn."

She grabbed his cock in her hand and slid her fist up and down the length of it. He rolled onto his back with a sigh, and Bea dusted kisses down his sides and impossibly hard stomach until he squirmed.

"Jesus, Bea."

She grinned as she wrapped her lips around his shaft and slid her mouth down it. Aiden groaned, and she thrilled at the sound. He wanted her. He made that noise for her. And God was that hot.

Aiden wrapped his hands in her hair as she licked and sucked more sexy and desperate noises from him.

"Shit, Bea. Stop." He ground out through clenched teeth. She sat on her heels, admiring him from her position between his thighs.

"Come here." He leaned against the headboard and she sat facing him, straddling his lap.

"Was it good?" She was nervous again, and he ran hands down her back, reassuring her.

"Too good. I didn't want this to be over yet." He ducked his head a little, not meeting her eyes, and she found this confession to be the sexiest thing he had said all night. He kissed her, his tongue exploring her mouth. She let him, then took his bottom lip between her teeth and nibbled it, fulfilling a lifelong dream.

His cock pressed against her center, and she rocked her hips against it. *Oh, that will work.* She did it again, harder and faster. Aiden met her gaze. He licked his bitten lip, his eyes dark with desire.

"Keep going," he whispered. "Make yourself come."

It was not an invitation she was about to turn down. She ground against him until she was moaning and panting. She gripped his shoulders hard enough to leave marks. The thought got her hotter. She came with a gasping shudder and leaned her forehead onto his chest.

"Fuck, that was hot." His mouth was everywhere, her lips, her cheeks, her neck. It was an all-out assault of kisses. His stubble burned her, and red blooms appeared on her pale skin. Good. Evidence to remind her it was real.

"I want you." She climbed off his lap and pulled him on top of her.

He paused above her. "Condom?"

She grimaced. "I don't have any." How little faith she had in her own plan. She didn't bring condoms. Unbelievable.

His face was a comical mask of faked calm. "Okay. That's okay." He pulled away.

Bea tugged him down. "I'm on the pill, and I'm clean."

"Me too. Clean, I mean. No pill."

She laughed underneath him, dragging him closer. She didn't trust anyone else to keep her safe. But Aiden, she trusted with her life. His body covered hers, and she felt small and protected and wanted. She wrapped her legs around his back and linked her ankles above his butt. He pushed into her, slowly, a pained hiss escaping his mouth as he sank in deeper.

When they were linked together, he paused and his eyes locked with hers. A sob welled up in her throat. The sensation of him inside her was so intense tears threatened to spill over. He rested his forehead gently against hers.

"You okay?"

She smoothed her hands over the ridges on his biceps and swallowed her tears. "Yes. So much more than okay."

He smiled against her lips as he kissed her and began moving, his pace excruciatingly slow.

Sex with Aiden McLean. A Christmas miracle.

He thrust deeper and she gasped. She dug her fingers into his damp skin, and he moved faster. His back muscles bunched and flexed beneath her hands.

"What do you need?" His voice was strained in her ear. No one had ever asked her that before.

What did she need? She needed this forever. She groaned as he rocked his hips into her again and again, her pleasure building with each stroke. She slid a hand between their bodies and rubbed where she needed extra friction. Aiden grinned and drove harder into her until her thoughts were liquid and her body was pure heat. The room dissolved around her and another orgasm tore through her. She shook with it and moaned his name. She dropped her hand to the side, and Aiden came inside her with a shudder and his gasps tickling her ear.

He collapsed next to her and wrapped his arms around her. She was sleepy and sated and wanted nothing more than to enjoy the weight of his arm on top of her and his warm body next to her. But a small, terrifying question surfaced as she snuggled in closer. What now?

She was too afraid to ask.

Chapter Six

December 30, Present Day

The sun streamed in through the window, shining light on everything they did last night. Bea was curled up next to him, her hair a crown of blonde tangles. The sheets and blankets were wrapped around her small frame in a makeshift nest. She looked comfortable beside him. She looked like she belonged there.

Aiden ran a hand over his face. What had he done? Last night was amazing. And terrible. Both were objectively true. The sex was…the sex was…never mind the sex. Being with Bea was everything he imagined and more. And now he had to tell her it couldn't happen again.

No matter what she said last night, one night was not possible for Bea. Crossing this line with her had been a huge mistake, but one he was having a hard time regretting. They had already crossed so many other lines this week he lost track of why crossing this last one was a bad idea. Now in the clear light of day he remembered.

Aiden hadn't had a relationship last longer than a few months in his entire life. Even his mother knew he wasn't worth sticking around for. If he let this continue with Bea, there was no way he wouldn't disappoint her. And the deeper in they were when it happened, the harder it would be to dig themselves out.

"You're not sketching me?" Her voice was sleepy, and she spoke without opening her eyes. Seeing her like this made him want to see her like this every day.

"Should I be?"

She smiled and peeked an eye open. "I always imagined sex with an artist would involve them sketching me nude. Is that not customary?"

He huffed a small laugh. She was so fucking perfect. Beautiful and funny and sweet fucking everywhere. He groaned internally.

"That's part of the deluxe package."

"Damn it. Next time I'll go for the upgrade." She was fully awake now, stretching next to him, her arms above her head. She leaned over and snuggled against him, her body still naked under the sheets.

He retreated further to his side of the bed, and the smile dropped from her face. She sat and wrapped her arms around her knees, bracing herself. He hated that he was the one who made her need to.

He sighed and sat next to her, leaning against the headboard. He had to make her understand.

"Your parents came to my art show last year."

"What art show? You didn't tell us. I would have…"

He held up a hand. "That wasn't my point. I didn't tell anyone. I'm not sure how they found out about it. But they were there."

She studied his face for answers. What did she see when she looked at him? One thing was certain, her opinion of him was more than he deserved.

He went on, needing her to see. "And do you know who brought me to the hospital when my appendix burst?"

"Of course. It was James. It's one of his favorite

stories."

"Yeah, but did he tell you he slept in my hospital room while I recovered?"

She opened her mouth and closed it again, no words escaping. She clutched the blankets to her chest as though they were her protection from what came next.

"And every year, this week, here with you and your family. It's the best week of the year. It's my one week of…of…family." He dragged his gaze to meet hers. Her eyes shimmered with tears. Hurting her was inevitable. Lessening the damage was his best option. *Rip off the bandage.*

"I care about you, Bea. And I love your family more than my own. I can't risk losing any of you."

"But Aiden…" Her voice wavered as she tried to grab his hands, but he kept them in his lap. Touching her made him want to touch her forever. *Impossible.*

"Please. Tell me we can go back to normal." He was nearly begging her now. "Please tell me I didn't fuck everything up between us."

She swallowed hard. "So last night was a mistake?"

"No." He nearly shouted the word, and Bea flinched. Last night was far from a mistake. It had been the best night of his life. He moved toward her and cupped the side of her face in his hand. It took all his strength not to kiss her down-turned lips. "Last night was perfect. Do you regret it?" He had no right to ask her, but he needed to know.

"No." Her voice was a choked whisper.

He stroked her cheek with his thumb one last time and pulled his hand away. "But I can't. This can't happen again." He was afraid she might argue but she didn't. "I don't have anyone else." His voice cracked, and he hated how pitiful he sounded. But it was true. He rarely admitted it, but he had no one else. A few friends, of course. Some coworkers from the bar. But the people in this cabin were the only people in the world he loved. The risk was too great.

She twisted her hands in the blanket, her brow furrowed. For a minute it seemed she might let it go. But when her blue eyes met his again, she saw right through him.

"Why are you so convinced it won't work out? Why are you skipping to our breakup before you give us a chance?"

He shook his head, wishing they had gotten dressed before having this conversation. "Most relationships don't last, Bea," he told her, frustrated she made him say it. "Maybe if you didn't read so many books with half-naked men on the cover and watch so many sappy holiday movies, you would get it."

Her eyes widened. His comment was a low blow, but it was for the best. This insult, this minor fight, would heal quicker than the devastation of a breakup. It had to. The fear that she might hate him forever slid into his stomach and settled there, churning his insides into a toxic soup.

She paused, swallowing hard. Her chest heaved with every breath and her cheeks flushed red. He bit down hard on his bottom lip, repressing an apology. Angry Bea was better than hurt Bea.

She stood with the sheets still wrapped around her.

"Maybe you're right." She rolled her shoulders back, refusing to let him see her break. But Bea was one of the few things he was an expert on. And this wasn't a minor fight. It was already too late for that.

"Maybe I am naive or stupid for thinking happy endings are possible."

He opened his mouth to protest. He never meant to call her stupid. But she continued.

"But I feel sorry for you, Aiden. We're good together." She sniffed and wiped a tear from her cheek with her free hand. "You see it too. But you are too much of a coward to even try."

With this last knife to his heart, she turned and left the room.

****

"So how was it?" Camille's toes were a warm brown next to her pale white ones. She painted the nails a shimmery violet. Bea's were scarlet.

Bea shrugged, attempting to make her voice casual, unaffected. "Well, he made me come three times and then broke my heart. So, it was a bit of a mixed bag."

Camille frowned, the lines creasing her forehead. "Does he know how you feel about him?"

"I made it pretty clear last night."

She shook her head, her tight black curls swishing across her shoulders. "You made it clear you wanted to jump his bones, but did you tell him you're in love with him?"

Bea stilled, the tiny paintbrush hovering over her toes. Of course she hadn't told him. "No," she mumbled. "But, Cami, I can't. He doesn't want to be with me. Telling him I love him would have made things worse."

Camille huffed. "He needs to hear it." She capped the nail polish and laid back on the bed, keeping her feet firmly planted to avoid smears. Bea finished her last pinky toe and joined her, leaning against the headboard.

She tried not to remember the things she had done

up against this headboard but she failed. The images of last night played on a tortuous pornographic loop in her head. Her stomach heated in embarrassment every time Aiden's stinging rejection crossed her mind. But she knew Aiden. She wasn't the only one affected by what happened last night. Aiden's morning-after panic aside, things had changed between them forever.

"I'll avoid him until New Year's. After that, we can all return to our normal lives and pretend this never happened." Who was she kidding? Forgetting was not an option.

Camille turned to admonish her further, but James burst through the door without a knock.

"The cookies." He grinned and waved a yellowed piece of paper triumphantly above his head. Bea and Camille swiveled their heads toward the door, but neither bothered to sit up.

"What are you talking about?"

"The cookies. The magic Christmas cookies." He placed an exasperated hand on his hip. "You want Aiden to eat them, of course. And here is the recipe." He laid it on the bed with a flourish.

Bea straightened against the headboard, careful of her toes. "Well, you're about twenty-four hours too late."

"What do you mean? I saw the way he looked at you last night at dinner. And he told me you kissed. What's the problem?"

She groaned and flung herself into the pillows again, so Camille explained. "They had sex last night." She paused for James's dramatic gasp. "But then he told her they can't do it again."

James grimaced. "Yikes. That bad, huh?" Bea launched a pillow at his face. He ducked, and it hit the wall behind him.

"What did he say exactly?"

"It's your fault," Bea growled at him from her nest of pillows.

"How is it my fault?" James's eyes went comically wide at the accusation.

She struggled upright again and glared at her brother. "He said he's too close to our family, and you're like his brother, and he doesn't want to lose any of us. He thinks if we try something and break up, he wouldn't get to be part of our family anymore." Her voice cracked. He had looked so sad when he said it. There was no way to argue. No way to ask him to risk the people he cared about for her. Especially when he was so convinced things would end in disaster.

James sighed and pinched the bridge of his nose. "That's ridiculous. Obviously, I would pick him over you in the breakup," he teased.

"Shut up." She was not in the mood for her brother's jokes.

"He's scared, Bea." He said it like it was the most obvious thing in the world. She remembered calling Aiden a coward this morning with the sudden feeling she was about to regret it.

"Do you know why he spends Christmas with us?"

She wiped her eyes with her hand. "Yeah, he doesn't want to fly to California every year. And he doesn't get along with his mom's new family."

James shook his head. "That's part of it." He sat on the end of her bed, settling in when all Bea wanted was to be alone to wallow.

"What does any of this have to do with us being together?"

"One of the first times Aiden and I got drunk together, he told me a lot of stuff about his family. Actually, it's a funny story. We were at this party off campus…"

"Good lord, James," she snapped. "Get on with it. Tell me what I need to know." Her brother loved to drag out a story, and she did not have time right now. Cami stifled a laugh.

"Okay, okay. Don't get your panties in a twist."

She stuck her tongue out at him, and he returned the gesture but mercifully got to his point.

"Growing up, anytime Aiden got in trouble, his mom told him he was so much like his father. His whole life she compared him to the one person who hurt her the most."

Her throat tightened at the image of a little Aiden being told he was like his absent dad. She had the sudden urge to find his mother and slap her.

"Add that to the fact he is now the spitting image of his dad. I've seen pictures." James shrugged. "He's convinced he will hurt you, like it's in his DNA or something."

"Shit." It was so much easier to be pissed at him before she had this information. "What am I supposed to do now?"

"The only thing you can do. Show him how to be brave." He patted her knee and left the cookie recipe on the bedside table. "Oh, and feed him the cookies."

Butter Cookies. The title was scrawled in her grandmother's handwriting on a scrap of notebook paper, letters missing from where spilled liquids had washed away the ink. Bea ran her finger over the ingredients: butter, sugar, flour, eggs, vanilla, and salt.

She had a feeling it was going to take more than baked goods to convince Aiden they were worth the risk.

Chapter Seven

New Year's Eve, Present Day

"But you're going to miss game night!"

She gave her brother a withering stare. "James, this is more important than game night."

He continued pouting but helped her stuff her clothes into her duffle bag. "Sure, I get that, but with you and Aiden both gone, there's no real competition left. It will be a massacre."

Bea zipped her bag and hurried from the room, James on her heels. Her parents waited for her in the living room. "Okay, I'm leaving."

They all stared at her. By the pitiful looks on their faces, one would think she was leaving them forever instead of missing one New Year's Eve. "Guys, it's not a big deal." She shrugged on her coat. "I can't let him leave without saying anything. I need to at least try to fix things between us."

Her mother handed her a tin of cookies. Bea didn't have to open the lid to know what was inside. "Mom, it's a little late for these."

"Late for what?" Her mother had a horrible lying face. It was half the reason game night was bound to be a disaster. She had zero ability to bluff. "You might need a snack for your drive." She added a casual shrug for good measure.

Bea sighed and placed a hasty kiss on her cheek and turned to her father.

"Tell him he's still family."

"Okay, Dad, will do." A kiss for her father and she was out the door.

"Make sure you fix my best friend." James's voice broke through the still evening as she hustled to her car. "You broke him."

Bea turned to see his teasing smile, but James's joke hit a little too hard. Had she broken Aiden? Had she ruined what they had by trying to get more? She huffed another sigh and threw her bag into the back seat, tossing the tin of cookies next to her in front.

Aiden had left early enough this morning that by the time she was awake, he was already gone. Nothing but a note to the family explaining he had to cover for someone at work. Aiden hadn't worked on New Year's Eve in ten years.

He was running away. Running away from her. And it sucked. She needed to tell him the truth before he decided not to be with her. The entire truth, the things she hadn't been brave enough to say. And if he still didn't want her, she at least needed him to know his place in her family was secure.

It took her most of the day to gather enough courage to go after him and late afternoon quickly turned to dusk as she pulled out of the driveway. Pink and lavender light colored the snow as she left town and turned onto the highway.

Her phone buzzed, rattling the cupholder, and her heart leaped into her throat. But the name glowing on the screen was Grandma Rose, not Aiden. Bea put her on speaker.

"Hey, Grandma."

"Hi, sweetie. I'm glad you answered. Are you driving? I don't want to distract you."

"It's fine, Grandma. You're on speaker."

"I'm on speaker, Patrick." Bea waited for her grandparents to finish arguing in the background about whether or not it was safe for her to talk and drive.

"Listen, honey, I'm going to make this quick. Your grandfather is worried you're going to drive off the road."

Bea smiled at her grandmother's aggrieved voice.

"I wanted to wish you luck with Aiden."

Jesus, did everyone know about her love life? Was there a phone tree everyone was on? "Thanks, Grandma."

"He's a nice boy."

"Yes, he is."

"Handsome."

"Very."

"Do you have the cookies?"

Bea glanced over to the seat beside her. The legend of the magic Christmas cookies seemed more and more ridiculous by the minute. "I don't think the cookies are going to help this time. He was pretty freaked out last I saw him."

"Yes, I asked about the cookies!" Her grandmother did not bother to move the phone away from her face as she yelled at her grandfather, and Bea was glad she wasn't holding it to her ear. "Well, don't lose faith now, honeybee."

"Okay. Thanks, Grandma. I should concentrate on the road."

"I will let you go, but tell him how you feel."

"Yes, Grandma."

"And feed him the cookies."

"Okay, Grandma. Love you. Bye."

Bea sighed. Her entire family was insane. The man she loved fled the scene after they had sex, but sure, cookies would fix everything.

It was an hour's drive to Boston from the cabin. Bea barely had enough time to switch from wallowing in self-pity to rehearsing what she was going to say before she entered the city limits.

For a minute, she considered driving to her apartment instead, pouring a glass of wine, and pretending this whole thing never happened. Aiden had left for a reason, and maybe he was right. But she had come this far; she might as well drive the nail into her own coffin and lay it all out there. What else did she have to lose?

She took the exit to Winter Hill. Bea had never been to Aiden's apartment, had never been invited. But her mother had the address. The fact he lived in Somerville, across the Charles River from her apartment in Boston, added insult to injury. He had spent a lot of years avoiding her.

The GPS claimed her destination was on the right, but all she saw was a liquor store and a Brazilian restaurant. Bea peered at the dingy building and realized Aiden must live over the liquor store. Of course, he did. Her starving artist. A string of Christmas lights hung over the shop window and a silver tinsel wreath hung on the door in a failed attempt at festivity.

Bea pulled into the lot on the side of the building. She could do this. Be honest. And don't forget the cookies.

****

Aiden was halfway through his second beer when a knock on the door interrupted the lengthy one-sided argument he had been having in his head since he fled the cabin this morning. His rescue cat, Winston, looked at him in surprise.

"I'm not expecting anyone. Are you?"

Winston didn't crack a smile. Aiden gave him a quick scratch between the ears on his way to the door.

He glanced around, making sure things weren't in too much of a disastrous state before he answered. It was a studio apartment. Anytime he opened the door, his entire life was on display. His bed was still unmade, but clear of anything besides blankets and pillows. His easel and paints filled the corner where a kitchen table might have gone, but at least the paintings were neatly stacked against the wall.

Two strides and he was through the galley kitchen. The sink was clear of dishes and the counters clean since he hadn't been home in days. The plants in the window looked a little grim, but with a bit of watering, they'd come back to life.

Satisfied, he pulled the door open, half expecting to see the manager from downstairs asking him to lock up so he could cut out early. But it wasn't Len. It was the last person he expected to see.

"Bea." Her name left his lips in a rush of air.

"Hi." She didn't smile. Her usually bubbly voice was all business.

"Hi." He had forgotten how to speak. Echoing her seemed to be all he was capable of.

She looked at him expectantly as she stood in the hall, the liquor-soaked air wafting up from below.

Winston meowed around his feet. He had no choice but to let her in.

"Sorry, come in." He stood aside and Bea floated in, filling his apartment with her sweetness. "Uh…what are you doing here?"

"What are you doing here?" she countered. "I thought you got called into work." She wasn't looking at him but instead scanning his small space. It wasn't much. He was painfully aware of that. But he liked it. The sun was perfect in the morning for painting. He walked everywhere he needed to, and Len gave him a sizable discount on booze. But how did Bea see it?

She finished her tour and smiled in satisfaction. "I like your place."

"Oh?" His shoulders relaxed at the approving tone in her voice. "Thanks."

She squatted down to pay proper attention to Winston's upturned belly, and he purred in satisfaction.

"But you're not off the hook. Why did you leave?"

"Bea, can we not do this?"

She stood to face him, Winston meowing in protest. "Do what? Talk about what happened between us? You wanted things to go back to normal. But you left. That's not normal."

He needed room to move, but this damn apartment was too small. He shifted from foot to foot. "Is your family pissed?"

"No. But they want you there. And so do I."

"I thought it would be better if we had a little space after what happened." He cringed at the cliché. And it was a lie. Things were never better with space between them.

Bea narrowed her eyes. She still wore her coat and

boots, an enormous purse slung over one shoulder. If he offered to take her coat, she might stay. And that was something he both desperately wanted and feared at the same time. So he didn't offer.

"Aiden, why do you have a bee tattooed on your chest?"

It was not the question he expected from her. He hesitated, not able to think of a lie quick enough. The bee was a horrible mistake made in a fit of loneliness. He was at the tattoo shop to get color added to a zinnia on his arm but instead asked for a "B" on his chest. He wanted her engraved on his skin, as close to his heart as possible. The tattoo artist misunderstood, and he ended up with a small fuzzy bumblebee flying across his chest. But somehow that worked too.

"I like bees." He shrugged.

She took a step closer, trapping him in his own tiny kitchen. "I don't think that's why."

"Bea…"

"I'm in love with you." The words flew from her mouth and struck him with the force of a punch to his tenderest places.

"You're what?"

"I'm in love with you. I needed to tell you."

He opened his mouth to protest but she kept going, the words spilling out of her. "I know you're worried about what will happen if this doesn't work out, but what if it does? It's worth the risk, Aiden. I'm in love with you, and I think you're in love with me, too."

She stopped, breathless. And those words, I'm in love with you, buzzed all around him and lodged in his heart. Her face was so hopeful and honest and open. It gutted him.

"I can't do it, Bea." His voice cracked. "I will hurt you and I can't do that."

"Why?" She stepped closer and grabbed two fistfuls of his shirt, hanging on like he might bolt out the door at his back. "Why are you so convinced you will hurt me?"

He nearly laughed. Had she forgotten that he already had?

"What if I'm like him?"

"Aiden, you are not your father."

"Well, my mother seems to think so." His voice was raw and jagged. He had never said those words aloud. "She can't even stand to be in the same room with me. All she sees is him."

Bea loosened her grip on his shirt, and spread her hands over his chest, soothing him. He ached to pull her closer but didn't dare.

"If you don't want to be like your father, don't be like him."

He blinked. "It's not that simple."

"It is that simple." She pushed away from him, moving further into the apartment. She ran a hand over his latest painting, an abstract swirl of colors and textures he had done while thinking of her. Always while thinking of her. "You left today instead of talking to me. You were afraid of becoming your father, but you did exactly what he did."

She pulled his guts out and laid them in front of him, showing no mercy. Who was this Bea?

"Don't leave next time. I want you. I want you to stay. And for the record, so does my entire family." She turned and waited for him to respond. "If you can honestly tell me you don't want to be with me, then say it. Say it and I will let this go forever. But you'll always be part of my family."

He wanted it to be simple. He was tired of being afraid. And of being alone. If she was willing to take a risk on him, he needed to be brave enough to let her. Wasn't one more night with her, one more second, worth whatever pain might follow?

There were words he needed to say, proclamations he wanted to make, but he didn't trust his voice. So instead, he crossed his apartment, grabbed Bea's face in his hands, and kissed her, telling her everything with his lips instead of his words. She groaned his name against his mouth. Her hands raked through his hair and he pulled her closer, deeply regretting not taking her coat earlier. She shimmied out of it now, her mouth never leaving his.

Gasping for air, she pulled away. "Stop."

He stilled, resting his forehead on hers. His heart crashed against his ribs. Her eyes flicked up, brilliant blue even in the dim light of his apartment.

"I can't…if we do this…" She hesitated. It was his turn to be brave.

"It's for you." Everything he'd thought about her for the last seven years clamored to get out of his head, but he started with this. "The bee on my chest, it's for you."

"Oh." The word was a small sigh on her perfect lips.

"It's for all the times I missed you and all the times I couldn't tell you how I felt about you. I wanted you close to me and I thought…" He paused, and she brushed an encouraging kiss across his lips.

"And I convinced myself this was the only way I could have you."

"Aiden." His name on her lips was all he needed to hear.

"I want you, Bea. I've wanted you for years and it never seemed possible. I was afraid I'd hurt you."

"You won't," she whispered. He envied her conviction, her faith in him. Everything in him yearned to prove her right. No more running away from her. No more hiding behind his excuses.

"If we do this, I'm all in."

The smile that broke out across her face made him wonder how he had ever attempted to live without it. She pulled him closer, her arms still around his neck, and brought her mouth to his.

"I'm so glad." She grinned against his lips.

He kissed her, his arms wrapped around her waist, pulling her tight against him. They broke apart long enough to shuck off unnecessary clothing, then he kissed her again, devouring her. She sighed and moaned and whimpered, and he relished every sound. He backed her up to the bed until they both tumbled into it.

She kissed and nipped along his neck as he braced over her. She ran her fingers along his back, and he shivered under her touch. He dipped his head and sucked on the tender skin of her neck until she arched against his chest.

"Now, Aiden. I want you now."

He pulled away, rolling onto his side next to her. He loved how she looked beside him, her cheeks pink with desire and her golden hair fanned out around her. She looked like a debauched angel. He wanted to paint her like this. A wicked smile curved his lips.

Bea raised an eyebrow as though reading his mind. He didn't give her a chance to ask before he ran a hand down her stomach, tracing her curves. She gasped. Her back bowed when he brought his hand lower, finding her where she was hot and ready. He circled her there, achingly slow at first, then faster until she writhed next to him.

"Aiden, please…" She tugged on his shoulder. "I want all of you."

"You have all of me," he whispered, nuzzling her ear. He rubbed her harder until she screamed his name.

"Jesus Christ," she mumbled as he kissed down her shoulder, his filthy-talking, debauched angel. "More," she added, tugging him on top of her.

She wrapped her legs around him, and he buried himself inside her. She purred in his ear, and he nearly came from that alone.

"Shit, Bea." He rocked against her and she moaned. "I need you deeper."

He pulled out and rolled her onto her stomach. She lifted her perfect ass as he slid back into her warmth, reaching deeper than before. He kissed along her neck, twining his fingers with hers as she dug them into the mattress. She cried out beneath him as he thrust harder and faster, hitting exactly where she needed him to.

When she came apart, he held tight to her and followed her over the edge.

He collapsed next to her, raining kisses across her shoulders and face. She was fucking perfect, and she was his.

****

New Year's Day, Present Day

Bea woke to the sound of crunching. She peeked an eye open to find she was still in Aiden's bed, and miraculously, he was still beside her.

"Good morning." His voice was gruff from sleep. He cleared his throat.

"Morning." Bea propped herself up in bed. "What are you eating?"

Aiden held up the tin of her grandmother's Christmas cookies. "These fell out of your bag. I assumed they were for me since you've been trying to fatten me up on cookies all week." She winced, but he smiled and popped another cookie in his mouth.

There was a sketch pad on Aiden's lap. The morning sun slanted across the page. Bea recognized the lines of her arm and part of her face. "Were you sketching me?" She craned her neck for a better look, but he held it out of her reach.

He ducked his head, his cheeks pinkening. "I haven't done figure drawing in a long time. But you deserve the upgraded package." He grinned and tugged away the sheet she was wearing. "It's better without this though."

Bea laughed and snatched the sheet, bringing Aiden with it. He kissed her, and she tasted the cookies on his lips.

"So, what was with all the cookies this year anyway?"

Her lips twitched. Everything was out on the table now. She might as well tell him. "I was looking for the magic cookies."

Aiden's eyebrows rose to his hairline. "Excuse me, the what?"

"The magic cookies that make people fall in love. I'm sure we've told you the stories before."

"Oh right, the magic Christmas love cookies." He held one between his fingers, contemplating. "I'm not sure about magic."

"No?"

He put the tin of cookies aside and tossed his sketchbook off the bed. He moved in closer and kissed along her bare shoulder until she dropped the blankets. His gaze met hers.

"But I am sure I love you. And it has nothing to do with cookies."

Chocolate Chip Christmas Wishes

by

Nicole McCaffrey

Christmas Cookies Series

Dedication

For the real Kim, Laura, Pam and Sarita who make me laugh and cheer me on every day.
Merry Christmas, my friends.

Acknowledgements

Editor Kayce John –thank you for everything.

Chapter One

The North Pole

A pounding outside resonated in time with the hammering in Jake Mistletoe's temples. He twitched and tried to sit up, but the freight train chugging through his head made movement impossible.

Forcing open heavy, gritty eyelids, he gazed at the familiar carpet and recognized the pile of discarded clothes below him as his own. When had he passed out on the sofa? And why was he naked?

Tap, tap. Tap, tap, tap.

Not pounding so much as the sound of someone knocking on glass.

Like a window or... *Aw hell. The snow globe.*

He grabbed a nearby blanket to cover his lower half as the orb on the coffee table began to glow a bluish white, bringing a familiar image to light.

"Good morning." Despite the pleasant greeting, his mother sounded anything but friendly.

He dropped his cheek back onto the sofa cushion and groaned. "What time is it?"

A bright flash made him squeeze his eyes shut tight. A whiff of vanilla and cinnamon and the jingle of bells told him she'd arrived via the Elf Transport System. "Time you grew up, that's what time it is."

He struggled onto an elbow and attempted to push

up. His stomach heaved, and his mother's red and green booted foot appeared before his vision, pushing a wastebasket in front of his face just in time.

"Aren't you getting a little old for this?" she asked after his stomach had emptied itself.

He'd been on the receiving end of this conversation enough times to know there was no answer that would discourage the lecture.

"You're almost thirty, Jake. How much longer do you plan to carry on like some overgrown frat boy?"

He flopped onto his back, placing an arm over his eyes against the blinding daylight. "Will you make me some gingerbread tea?" He did his best to sound pitiful, hoping she'd soften and prepare her famous hangover remedy for him.

"No, I will not."

Boy, she sounded pissed. He opened one eyelid halfway to see her bend down to pick up discarded bottles, cans and clothing. She straightened, a lacy purple bra dangling from one finger. "Who does this belong to? Flora—or Fauna?"

From over his mother's shoulder, he caught sight of a similar scrap of lace—this one in vibrant red—draped over a lampshade. It didn't really matter which twin it belonged to; he'd been with both last night. But there were certain things a guy didn't say to his mom.

Merry tossed the bra aside with a shake of her head. "Why you couldn't have given poor Gale a chance. True, she's a bit forceful, but she's strong and direct and…"

"Cold," he finished, an image of the oldest of Jack Frost's daughters coming to mind, causing a shudder. Strong and forceful didn't cover it, the woman was built like a lumberjack and had the warmth of an iceberg.

"Yes, well, she takes after her mother," Merry said absently. "But those sisters of hers…"

At the mention of the Frost twins, a grin played at one corner of his mouth. Fuzzy memories returned. Oh yeah, *that* was how he'd come to be naked on the couch…

He jumped when his mother delivered a stinging slap to the back of his head. "Get up, get dressed and get to work."

Geez, she was really fired up today. He struggled to sit.

"All these years, Nick has never said a word. Not one word." The bells on the toes of her boots jingled as she paced across the room, russet curls bobbing beneath her red and green hat. "He treats you as if you were his own son and how do you repay him? By behaving like the spoiled man-child you are." The sound of empty beer cans hitting the wastebasket punctuated every syllable. "You are not reliable, you are not responsible, you're barely even a grown-up at this point."

"That's not true, I'm the manager of the gift wrap department. You don't get a job like that by being irresponsible."

"And the fact that your mother is head elf had nothing to do with that?" The sarcastic tone warned she wasn't through arguing. She picked up empty wine glasses and headed toward the kitchen. "Nick and Nora have been so good to us. They took us in as if we were family after your father and I…"

Jake wiped a hand down his face. "You mean after you erased his memory?"

He felt rather than saw her stop in her tracks and instantly regretted the reminder. If they so chose, elves could visit the real world when they came of age. The hope was after tasting life in the outside world, they would return to the North Pole. Sometimes their true identity was discovered, though, and measures were taken to erase the memories of those they'd encountered.

Jake, however, had yet to make such a journey. And why would he? Life at the North Pole was great. He had his own place, good job, fast snowmobile, all the video games, gadgets and toys any guy could want. And with perks like the Frost twins as playmates, why would he want to leave?

Merry returned from the kitchen, a distracted frown on her face. "You know when I left your father, I had no idea about…that I was…"

"Pregnant," he finished for her, eager to end the story lest she launch into it for the millionth time.

"Nick has been more than patient waiting for you to grow up and decide what role you want to have around here." She bent to pick up his jeans and tossed them at him. "It's not like they had children of their own. He's counting on you to step up and take on more responsibility."

Jake sighed, mouthing along as she spoke words he'd heard more times than he could count.

"It's about time you went out into the real world yourself." Merry put her hands to her hips, nodding as if she'd just decided something important. "Maybe then you can decide where you belong." She whirled to face him.

"Do you mind?" He held the jeans over his lower half and gestured for her to turn around. She did—and released a groan of disgust as she spied the red bra and snatched it from the lamp shade.

He grabbed his tee shirt from the floor and shrugged into it, slid into his jeans and zipped up. "What do you mean 'decide where I belong'?"

She turned to face him. "You've never had the chance to choose, Jake. And I know you…struggle to fit in."

"Maybe because everyone here is two feet shorter than I am?"

Merry bit her lip, green eyes welling as she studied him. "It's more than that. I think you have the right to know what life is like in the human world. It was elfish of me not to encourage you to go. You never seemed ready. But you are half human, after all, and more than old enough."

He sighed, eager for this conversation to end so he could grab some aspirin, a large coffee and head to his office for a long nap. "So, what are you saying? I can't go now, it's only a few weeks till Christmas, it will have to wait until after the new year."

She waved a hand and a duffel bag appeared at his feet. A shock of panic shot through him. Was she serious? A glance at his mother's face, mouth set in a determined grimace, chilled him to the bone.

"If I wait for you to decide, you'll never do it. Christmas is six weeks away. I'll need you back here by mid-December, so you have thirty days, Jake. I'll check in with you then."

She raised both hands and wiggled her fingers. Electricity from the snow globe arced toward him in a blinding blue-white flash.

"Wait, I'm not—"

In the blink of an eye, everything familiar disappeared.

Nicole McCaffrey

Chapter Two

Christmasville, NY

"—wearing shoes."

Lucy Prescott raised an eye from her cellphone. She didn't recall a guy standing there when she'd come out of the coffee shop and walked to the corner a moment ago.

Bing Crosby crooned *White Christmas* from tinny outdoor street speakers, but even over that noise, she could have sworn the guy in front of her had just talked to himself.

The "walk" icon had yet to appear on the crosswalk sign and he didn't seem to notice he was halfway into the street.

Should she say something? He didn't look like a homeless person. But he wore only jeans and a tee shirt on this cold, wet November morning. And no shoes. She shook her head. Probably out of his mind on drugs.

A quick glance around showed the others waiting for the light to change had noticed him, too, but rather than interact with another human being, most returned their attention to their cell phones.

She made eye contact with a man across the street wearing a cheap Santa suit and ringing a bell beside a red bucket. He nodded toward the drugged-out guy in the street and gave a "whaddaya gonna do?" shrug. She rolled her eyes and looked away.

It was way too early for the Red Kettle campaign and "Santa's" bucket was lacking any charity logo. But caught up in the atmosphere of a town like Christmasville, where it was Christmas all year long, tourists dropped money in the bucket without thought.

The guy staggered farther into the street, muttering something about filing a complaint with the elf union.

The gasp and hiss of air brakes sounded in a shrill whistle as a tourist shuttle rounded the corner, heading their way. Damn. The guy was right in the path.

"Hey mister," she yelled, "You might want to—"

But he wasn't listening, instead he turned a slow circle, oblivious to the honking horns as he stepped ever nearer to traffic, mouth gaping open as if he'd never seen Main Street before.

"Dude! There's a bus coming!"

With only a split-second left, she launched herself into the street and shoved him into the empty middle lane. Horns blared. The screech of brakes and the crunch of metal exploded. She braced herself for impact, held her breath and waited for the pain.

Nothing.

She raised her head. Three cars had crashed into each other to avoid hitting the druggie-pedestrian. Probably not the smartest move, pushing him into the turn lane, but she'd had no other option. Hot liquid seeped onto the leg of her jeans, warming her thigh. Damn. Her peppermint mocha latte right down the sewer. On the pavement beside her lay her cell phone, an ugly crack spiderwebbing across the now-dark screen.

She pushed herself to a sitting position. "Crap."

Beneath her, the drugged guy groaned but made no

attempt to rise.

"Mister, are you all right?"

He put a hand to his forehead and moaned. "Where the hell did she send me?"

Judging from the smell of his breath, alcohol, rather than drugs, had him so out of it. Lucy resisted the urge to judge even as she recoiled. She reached around him to pick up her cell phone and caught a whiff of something…amazing.

What was that wonderful scent that suddenly made her feel all warm and happy inside? It smelled like… like…

Chocolate chip cookies.

Damn if he didn't smell like fresh-baked chocolate chip cookies!

She bent to sniff his gray tee shirt and inhaled the pleasant aroma again. Wow. What they couldn't do with fabric softener these days…

"Did you just sniff me?" The voice, deeper than expected and slurred by his inebriated state, sounded sexy as hell.

By now a crowd had gathered and people rushed toward them from cars and businesses.

"Lucy!" Rick Williams, the owner of the coffee shop, ran toward her with a blanket. "Don't move, I've called the paramedics."

"I'm fine," she insisted, reaching out a hand for assistance in getting to her feet. The moment she tried, her ankle twinged. "But this guy is really out of it." She made a drinking motion with her hand and mouthed the word *drunk.*

Rick eased the man to a sitting position while Lucy wrapped the blanket around his shoulders. She'd intended to wait right here in the street for the paramedics, but Cookie Guy began to shiver. The coffee soaking her jacket and jeans was no longer warm; the cold was seeping into her, too.

"Maybe we should take him inside," Rick suggested.

Together they managed to get him to his feet. She was grateful for the older man's help in hoisting the guy up since putting weight on her ankle was painful. Together they hobbled the short distance to the opposite curb.

"My shop is probably closest." Lucy dug in her coat pocket for her keys. "Let's take him there."

Sleigh bells gave a merry jingle as she unlocked the door and held it open with a hip while Rick helped the man inside. "Over there, near the fireplace, on the sofa."

She'd only just put out that display, it involved a life-sized snoozing Santa, but she hadn't pulled it out of storage yet. She switched on the light and the soft glow of holiday bulbs bathed the room. The little mechanical elves and reindeer, relics from when her grandparents had opened the shop in the sixties, began their decades-long ritual of sawing wood and painting ornaments.

They'd done little more than settle Cookie Guy on the sofa when the paramedics arrived.

He was still pretty out of it as they worked on him, asking him things like how much he'd had to drink, if he'd taken any illegal substances. He seemed more annoyed than injured, insisting he just wanted to sleep.

Once they'd determined there were no signs of a head injury, they focused on wrapping Lucy's ankle. They advised her to follow up with an urgent care center if it wasn't better in a day or so and recommended rest, ice, compression, and elevation. Well, with any luck she might be able to manage one of those today.

Much to her dismay, they didn't take the guy to the hospital. He'd refused and she knew the paramedics were not allowed to force him against his will. But he didn't seem in any hurry to move. In fact, he curled into a ball on the couch like a contented cat taking a mid-morning, pre-lunch nap. Rick returned to the street to gather the duffel bag Cookie Guy had been carrying and brought it in.

It really wouldn't be great for business, having some hungover man snoring on the shop's sofa all morning, but there wasn't much else she could do. It wasn't peak tourist season yet, and Tuesdays were slow days anyway. Maybe it wouldn't cause much of a fuss.

"You sure you don't want me to stay?" Rick offered, frowning at her guest.

Lucy sensed her fatherly business neighbor worried for her safety. "If he wakes up and tries anything, I'll zap him with pepper spray. Promise."

A half smile played over the man's face. "Fair enough. But I think I'll send Madison over when she gets out of school. She can work here today while you take it easy on that ankle."

She nodded her thanks. The teenager didn't do much other than stare at her cell phone and answer "I dunno" to every customer question, but at least she'd be company.

The police were in, too, to check on Cookie Guy's identity and take her statement. His duffel bag didn't contain much, a snow globe that seemed miraculously undamaged, all things considered, and a pocket watch. There was no identification. She'd have to wait until he woke and started talking. For now, she tucked his bag beneath the counter, tossed a blanket over him and placed a red Santa hat on his head to help him blend in.

As the day wore on, a few customers straggled in, but none seemed to mind her guest. She kept the electric fireplace going to keep him warm and poked him every time his snoring grew too loud. More than one customer walking past him commented on the delightful cookie aroma.

Young Madison arrived a little after two, and Lucy was more than ready to be off her ankle. Rather than leave the girl alone with the stranger, she gave the teen enough money to buy lunch for all of them and sent her back out.

By the time it neared the six o'clock closing hour, Madison had gone back to the coffee shop to work on homework and Lucy began to wonder what she would do with her guest if he didn't wake soon.

The afternoon light was waning into evening when he finally stirred.

She studied him as he sat up. Unconscious, the several days' growth of stubble and mussed dark hair looked sloppy. But awake, that disheveled look gave him a devil-may-care aura. How had she missed the chiseled jaw line, the dark brows that framed eyes fringed with long, sooty lashes or the fact that he was drop dead gorgeous?

He looked around the room, wiped a hand over his face and turned a slow half circle on the couch, gaping at the racks of holiday ornaments, animated characters, motion-activated novelties and Santa figures that played Christmas tunes.

She cleared her throat to draw his attention. "Good

afternoon."

He pulled the Santa hat from his head and pulled a frown before tossing it aside.

For lack of anything else to say, she chose the standard, cheery greeting used by locals. "Welcome to Christmasville, where it's Christmas all year long."

He turned to her with eyes a startling shade of blue. "Let me guess. I died, and this is Hell."

Chapter Three

Why had Merry sent him *here*? If she wanted him to discover life outside of the North Pole, why choose a cheap imitation of a holiday theme town well past its prime?

The girl sitting near the cash register on the opposite side of the room seemed to expect an answer, or response of some kind. She was pretty in a cute, fresh faced way that he had never been particularly drawn to. Reddish blonde hair pulled back in a ponytail, oversized hoodie and jeans all gave off a "gave up a long time ago" vibe.

He pulled the blanket from his lap and noticed his feet were bare. Huh? Oh, that's right. He'd been in the middle of telling his mother—

"How are you feeling?" The girl reached for something under the cash register and tucked it into her hand.

"How did I come to be here?" he asked.

"Oh, that. You fell. I mean, well…I…pushed you."

"You *pushed* me?" Why didn't he remember any of this?

"Just to get you away from the bus. I don't normally go around…you know, shoving guys into oncoming traffic."

A fuzzy memory teased the edges of his brain. "You sniffed me."

Her cheeks pinkened in a way that was kind of

168

adorable. "Oh that." She gave what sounded like a forced laugh. "I thought I smelled cookies. It's weird, I know."

"I get that a lot." All elves smelled like cookies, even half-elves like him. So not weird at all, but probably not the best conversation starter. For the first time he noticed her foot, bound in some sort of beige wrap, and propped on a crate. "What happened?"

"Uh…" She glanced down at her ankle, ponytail swishing over her shoulder. "You kind of…landed on me."

"I did?" He took a quick inventory of slim legs and, from what he could tell under the bulky pink sweatshirt, some tantalizingly full breasts. "I'm sorry I wasn't awake to enjoy it."

Her startled expression turned to relief as the bells above the door jingled. A middle-aged guy and teenage girl stepped in. The man's gaze sought him out before landing on the redhead at the register. "Everything all right, Luce?"

Immediately, Jake recognized the challenge in the older man's expression. Tall, broad shouldered, and solid—like he kept himself in shape—probably in his late forties. The teenaged girl wore a bored expression, working a wad of gum for all it was worth, phone propped in front of her face.

"Everything is great, Rick," the redhead said. "I was just telling um…I'm sorry, I didn't get your name?"

"Jake." Sensing they wanted a last name, he glanced over the girl's shoulder to a packing box with a name stamped on it. "Holiday. Jake Holiday." He winced as the dumb name left his lips.

"Mister Holiday." The girl gestured toward him. "I was telling him how he came to be in my shop. Jake, this is my business neighbor, Rick Williams and his daughter, Madison. Rick helped me get you inside after you fell."

Jake rose and extended a hand, noting the other man's firm handshake and wary gaze.

"Nine in the morning is a little early in the day to be drunk, son, don't you think?"

Geez if it wasn't his mother, it was total strangers. "Uh…yeah." He rubbed a hand over the back of his neck. "About that. I…had kind of a long night. Long… weekend, really. Sorry."

"No need to apologize, I was young once, too." The man brought his hands to his hips. "Is there someplace I can drop you off? Luce here is getting ready to close up."

Luce, he assumed, was the girl with the propped-up foot.

"Where are you staying?"

Man, the guy was like a Chihuahua with a pant cuff in his teeth, no way was he going to let go. "I…honestly don't know. I'm kind of new in town. Not sure how I even got here, really." Trying to explain the ETS, Elf Transport System, probably wouldn't be the best place to start.

"Oh my God. You must have hit your head when I knocked you down." This from Luce, who had hobbled toward the door to flip the "Open" sign over, but now stood with a hand to her mouth. "I gave you *amnesia*!"

Chapter Four

Madison looked up from her phone and popped the pink bubble protruding from her mouth. "If he's got amnesia, how come he knows his name?"

Lucy limped toward her, giving her elbow a gentle squeeze. Her grandma and Madison's mom had both passed away around the same time a few years ago. She'd tried to take on a sisterly role to the younger girl, just as Rick seemed to have appointed himself Lucy's adopted father. "I'll explain later."

"'Kay."

Rick still had his hands on his hips, making it clear he considered himself in charge. Once a high school coach, always a high school coach she supposed.

"I'll drop you at the Reindeer Lodge on my way home, then, see if they can get you a room."

Madison popped another bubble with a loud snap. "There's a conference in town, remember? The lodge is full up. Barbara is catering a luncheon there tomorrow, I'm helping her."

"Look, I don't want to put anyone to any trouble, I'll just be on my way." This from Jake, who stood by, looking like he'd rather be anyplace else.

"You aren't exactly dressed for the weather," Lucy pointed out, gesturing toward the window where a wet mix of snow and rain could be seen in the glow from the streetlights.

He glanced down at his bare feet.

"You often wander around without shoes, son?" Rick asked.

"No, no," Jake said, frowning. "I was getting dressed for work and…"

"Where do you work?"

Oh, this was bad. Rick was really grilling the guy.

"Uhh a factory. North of here."

Rick's hands were back on his hips. "Toronto? So you're Canadian?"

That made sense, they saw a lot of tourists from Canada, the border was only about an hour away. Maybe that's why he was so confused about where he was.

"Uh… a little farther North."

"Ahh, closer to Quebec then. Still, you're a long way from home with no place to stay tonight."

"Why can't he just stay here?" Madison asked in her usual bored tone.

"Here?" Lucy said it almost in time with Rick.

The girl looked up from her phone and shrugged. "Yeah. I mean Lucy has deadbolts on the door to the upstairs. The cash register is locked. And what's he gonna steal anyway, a bunch of Santa stuff? Besides the alarm would go off if he tried to leave."

Lucy glanced back toward the window, then to the barefoot guy standing before them. She chewed her lip, wondering if she should do as Madison suggested. A gust of wind picked up, rattling the window like it wanted to come in.

Those blue eyes, slightly bloodshot but nonetheless mesmerizing, landed on her face. She had the feeling he was weighing his options every bit as much as she.

Mind made up, she pulled in a steadying breath.

"There's a break room in back with a microwave and coffee maker. Powder room is off of that. I live upstairs but as Madison said, it's locked. I won't hesitate to call nine-one-one if I hear anything down here or if you try to come up."

Rick pulled himself up straighter. "I'm usually at my shop by five. I'll drive by to check on things before I head in."

She glanced at her friend, grateful for his concern but needing to make him understand she had this under control. "I'm sure it will be fine."

Cookie Guy's blue eyes continued to study her. A warm flush filled her insides. Under different circumstances, she could get used to looking at that face. A half grin turned up one corner of his mouth. "I'll be on my best behavior. Elf—I mean, scout's honor."

"So it's settled then?" Madison looked up from her phone again, this time turning to her father. "Can we stop by the store on the way home? For some reason I've been craving chocolate chip cookies all day."

Chapter Five

Long after the shops along the street had gone dark, Jake sat wide awake. Sleeping all day usually did that to him. The four cups of coffee he'd consumed in the hours since Lucy had gone upstairs probably didn't help.

Bored, he wandered about the tiny shop. More than once his attention drifted to the little animated characters in the front window. He turned on the lights, bathing the room in the glow of Christmas, and watched the little elves as they began to move.

He hadn't seen these relics around the factory in a long time. He studied them for a few moments. Their paint was chipped in places, and their movements were sticky, the gears grinding for a second before they snapped back.

When was the last time anyone had worked on them? Cleaned the parts, oiled the mechanisms, touched them up? He wished he had his tool kit from the workshop, he could fix them up in no time.

He drained his coffee cup again, intent on a refill when his toe bumped something on the floor. The duffel bag. He thought he'd left it over by the sofa. He lifted it, surprised to find it heavier than it had been earlier today. He set it down and heard the clink of metal.

She wouldn't…. would she? He unzipped the bag, grinning at the sight of his tool kit.

Merry had enchanted the bag. So whatever he

needed, he could get from here?

"How about some shoes?" he asked, half joking.

His favorite pair of Jordans appeared in the bag.

"Nice one." He pulled the sneakers out and slipped them on, wiggling his toes at the comfortable, familiar fit. "Great. Now how about a lift home?"

Nothing.

"A plane ticket? An Uber?"

Headlights cut across the room as a car moved down the street outside, a sprinkling of snow evident in the glow from the headlights. It slowed and for a split second, his heart lifted. The face of the guy who'd been in the shop yesterday—Rick, was it?—came into view, peering through the window, before moving along.

The bag remained empty. "Real funny, Mom."

He took the snow globe out and set it on the floor in front of him. There was no guarantee she was listening but just in case.

A glow inside the bag caught his eye and he reached in to find a golden pocket watch. He frowned. He didn't own one of these. Merry must have put it in the bag.

He flipped it open but instead of numbers it held a three-color gauge, like on a fuel tank. Green, yellow and red. Right now, the needle sat solidly on green.

He frowned and flicked a glance at the snow globe. "What are you up to?"

He reached for the bag again, finding it empty. "I wonder." He cleared his throat and looked back toward the snow globe, watching for any flicker of recognition. "I wish for a fifth of Jack Daniels and the Frost twins."

The needle on the gauge lurched forward, then snapped back. He looked around. No booze, no identical playmates.

"Okay, how about a six pack and *one* twin?"

Nothing.

"Well, I could at least use some socks and warmer clothes."

In an instant, the socks were on his feet and a sweater, tee shirt and his favorite leather jacket appeared on the sofa. A glance at the pocket watch showed the needle had edged over a fraction toward yellow.

"Now that's not fair, you're the one who sent me here with no warm clothes."

The snow globe glowed a blue white. "Ahh, so you *are* listening."

The needle on the pocket watch edged back. "I better not get penalized for the tool kit; I didn't officially ask for that." The needle moved back again.

The snow globe went dark. A strange sensation of loneliness assailed him. He'd never been entirely on his own before. Sure, he lived alone, and he liked to say he was a grown man, but in truth, he was surrounded by family most of the time. Hundreds of them. Elf first and second cousins and folks like Nick and Nora, who were not related but felt like family.

He sighed and fingered the pocket watch another moment. So the watch, not the bag, was enchanted? Either way he understood what it meant. Merry wanted him to be independent, not rely on elf magic—he possessed none of his own to begin with—to get by. Every time he used it, the gauge went down a little. What would happen if it ran out? Would he still be able to get home?

He decided not to dwell on that thought and reached for his jacket. He found a money clip with a few bills in the pocket. He had no idea how American currency worked but he'd bet it didn't amount to much. So she expected him to earn his way.

He picked up the sweater Merry had sent along with his jacket, frowning as he turned it to face him. On the front, a giant reindeer head with a flashing red nose stared back at him.

An ugly Christmas sweater.

"Very funny," he said to the dark snow globe. "We invented these."

****

Sleep proved elusive for Lucy, she tossed and turned half the night, thinking about the guy downstairs. Things were much too quiet down there.

Long before the sun rose, she was up and dressed. She took a bit more care with her hair and makeup today, chiding herself for bothering.

Okay, so he was kind of hot and it had been ages since she'd thought of anything but work or caring for her grandmother…a little lip gloss and mascara never hurt anyone. And maybe instead of her usual ponytail she'd wear her hair down.

A long sweater with a short denim jacket over it looked a little nicer than her usual hoodie. She couldn't do much about the shoes, not with her foot wrapped up, so she settled for a fuzzy slipper sock over the swollen foot and a cute flat on the other.

She locked up her apartment and thumped her way down the steps. Well, if he wasn't awake before this, he certainly would be now. The smell of a burnt coffee pot met her nose as she unlocked the door to the shop. She hurried into the breakroom to find the empty carafe left on the hot burner plate. Okay, so he liked coffee—and he was a bit irresponsible.

She set the pot aside to cool off and made her way into the shop. The lights were on, she always loved the soft glow of the twinkle lights in the early morning hours.

Loud snoring came from behind the couch. She peeked around to see him sprawled on the floor sound asleep. Surrounded by an assortment of tools, and her animated elf characters. Or rather, pieces of them.

She couldn't contain a cry of alarm. "What have you done?"

He sat up abruptly, looking around in confusion. "I didn't know she was your daughter."

"What?"

"What?" He shook his head. "I mean, good morning." He glanced toward the window. "Is it morning? I can't tell."

"Yes, it's a little past five." She gestured toward the mechanical elf slaughter on the floor. "Would you please tell me what these poor creatures did to deserve this?"

He wiped a hand down his face. "I'm fixing them. The gears are old—I don't have parts here to replace them, but I can rebuild the old ones."

She frowned. "Why would you do that?"

He chuckled and rose to his feet. "Boredom, I guess. It was a long night."

She folded her arms and looked pointedly at his chest. "Nice sweater."

He glanced down. "Yes, someone in my family must have a real sense of humor."

She walked across the room to flip the overhead switch. "That's funny. I thought when the police looked in your bag yesterday for ID it was empty except for the snow globe."

"What? No, the bag is full, see?" He grabbed the bag from the floor and unzipped it to show her a neatly folded stack of clothes and a toiletry kit.

"Hmmm, maybe I'm the one with amnesia," she said. "I could have sworn it was empty." She gestured toward the shiny tools on the floor. They were newer than anything her grandfather had left behind. "Were those in the bag, too?"

"Hmm? Uhhh…yeah. I always carry tools with me."

She laughed. "I can't wait till you remember all the details of how you got here, traveling with a duffel bag of clothes, a snow globe and tools."

****

The chill of the November morning bit into Jake as they stepped outside a short time later. He held the door while Lucy stepped out, eyeing the bright slipper sock on one foot. "Are you sure you should be walking around?"

"It's not far to the coffee shop, I'll prop it up when we get back."

As she stepped past him, the fresh clean fragrance of her hair filled his nostrils. A nice change from people who smelled like cookies.

"Mmmm, there it is again." She closed her eyes, and a smile lifted the corners of her mouth.

He placed a hand to her elbow. "Are you all right?"

She opened her eyes and stared up at him with a dazed expression. "Yes, but for a second—I don't know. I smelled cookies and remembered being in the kitchen with my grandmother. I think I was very young, but the memory is so clear. It was Christmas Eve, and we were making cookies for Santa."

"Undoubtedly why he has type two diabetes now," he mused.

She frowned at him. "What was that?"

"Just kidding." He forced a smile. Geez, he'd have to watch himself. As they walked on, he kept his pace slow for her. The street was quiet, only a few stragglers out at this hour. Probably shop owners heading to work. They all smiled and greeted her by name.

He studied the businesses as they passed by. The storefronts were old and dated, most looked like they were from the 70s with dark brown backgrounds and white lettering. The decorations lining the street had seen better years. The wreaths hanging from the streetlamps had faded to dull greenish browns; the velvet ribbons frayed at the edges. The whole thing gave off a "town that time forgot" vibe, and not in a good way.

"It didn't always look like this." The words were spoken so softly he barely heard them.

He cast her an apologetic look. "Sorry, was it that obvious?"

She glanced down. "It used to be one of the happiest places on earth. Before super stores and the Internet, I mean. This was the only place you could find Christmas every day of the year."

Well, maybe not the only place… He cleared his throat, keeping his steps slow to match hers. "So did you grow up here?"

"No. My grandparents lived here. It was my favorite place to visit, though. I lost my parents when I was in high school. After that, I came here to live."

"Here?" he asked. "Over the store?"

They reached the corner, and he pressed the button to wait for the *Walk* icon.

"No," she said, her voice thick with emotion. "They had a house just outside of town, like most of the other shop owners. But after my grandfather passed, the house was too much for Gran and me to take care of on our own."

The light changed and they stepped into the crosswalk. As they reached the other side, the smell of coffee filled the air.

"By then business had slowed down anyway," she continued. "We didn't see the tourists the way we had before and money got tight, so moving to live over the store made sense."

He couldn't think of anything to say to that. His life had been all about fun and games. He'd grown up spoiled and indulged, treated like a prince because of his mother's close friendship with Nick and Nora Claus. Guilt nagged at him to realize not everyone had it as good.

The sleigh bell over the door of the Jingle Java coffee shop rang as they stepped inside. A knot formed in his stomach at the sight of the guy from yesterday standing behind the counter.

Jake wasn't ready for another grilling, and he had no more answers to give the guy about where he was from and when he would leave. He glanced around at the wood furnishings and dark wood floor. Across the room two leather chairs sat before a crackling fireplace. It looked like the sort of place he'd head for coffee or a drink at the North Pole.

"Jake?" Lucy nudged him in the ribs. "He asked for your order."

"Uh…coffee. Black."

"Come on, you can do better than that," the guy teased. "How about the coffee of the day? It's my custom holiday blend, a light roast with just a hint of cinnamon, nutmeg and vanilla."

"Sure, sounds good." So…no twenty questions? Maybe he was too busy to bother with it today, though the shop only looked about half full.

The guy beamed a smile. "I think you'll like it. I call it the Merry Mistletoe blend."

For a second, it was like he'd hit the pavement all over again. The air seemed to be sucked out of the room. "The what?"

"Merry Mistletoe," Rick handed him a steaming cup. "I don't know, I took one whiff, and the name just came to me. Let me know what you think." He turned toward Lucy. "The usual for you, Miss Luce?"

"You know I can't resist your peppermint mocha lattes," Lucy said. "And two cranberry pumpkin muffins to go, please." The conversation faded to a buzz as Jake stepped across the room to stare out the window.

Merry Mistletoe? As in his mother's name? That couldn't be a coincidence.

So first he wakes up in some dead Christmas town. Then some guy just happens to serve him coffee with the same name as his mother?

He took a sip of the hot brew, wincing as it burned his tongue.

One thing was certain, the real Merry Mistletoe never did anything without a reason.

What the hell was she up to?

Chapter Six

Even in the November chill, heat from a series of small gas fireplaces set along the sidewalk and an overhead awning kept the outdoor seating area cozy. Rick had added it outside the coffee shop when he purchased it from the previous owners, making it a favorite spot for the locals.

Lucy sat in awkward silence picking at her muffin, studying the guy in front of her.

He looked around him, his expression both dazed and horrified at the same time. "So what is the point of all this?" he asked, swinging those baby blues back to her.

She flushed as a jolt shot through her at the visual contact. "It began just after World War Two and for a long, long time kids really believed this was where Santa and the elves lived." She took a sip of her latte, the flavors of peppermint and chocolate mingling on her tongue. "My grandparents moved here in the sixties as newlyweds, they both loved coming here as children— met here, in fact, and it was their dream to open a business and live here year-round."

She glanced at the quiet street that should have been bustling with tourists. Regret and sorrow mingled for what it had once been. "But in the last few decades kids have grown up so much faster and…I guess it's lost its appeal. Why travel here to visit Santa in person when you can follow him on social media every day?"

He nodded. "I get it. It's like that where I live, too."

"You remembered something." She smiled, brightening at the idea of his memory returning. A wave of sadness followed that thought. A guy as good looking as him probably had a girlfriend, great job…everything. And what did she have but a lot of lost dreams and a dying business? Once he remembered where he came from, he'd be gone.

"I guess I did." He nodded toward the little red and white candy cane striped house in the park across the street. "Is that it? The place where Santa supposedly lives?"

"Yes." She rose. "It has fallen out of use in the last ten years or so, but it's all still there. Would you like to see it?"

He glanced down at her foot. "Are you sure you're up for that?"

"I'm okay." In truth her ankle had begun to throb, but she would take some pain reliever when she got back to the shop and prop it up. He would likely be on his way soon and Wednesdays were notoriously slow around Christmasville, too late for those who took a long weekend and too early for the weekend crowds.

The thought of him leaving and her spending another long day puttering around the quiet shop alone sent a pang of loneliness through her as they rose and made their way to the corner again.

As they approached Santa Claus Lane with its bright red and white peppermint walkway and candy cane arches, she tried to see it through his eyes. The fiberglass house was chipped and cracked, the sidewalk leading up to it buckled in places and strips of paint hung from the sign overhead.

Off to one side a set of eight fiberglass reindeer stood before an empty sleigh. They, too, were chipped and weather worn. He approached the sleigh, running a hand over it in an almost reverent gesture. "I haven't seen this model in years."

She frowned. "Model of what?"

He glanced at the paint chips on his hand and brushed it down his jeans. "The sleigh. It should be more modern; I doubt Santa has used anything like this in fifty years or more. It should be enclosed and there should be a heater, a navigation system, Bluetooth. Not to mention." He thumped the back of the seat. "It's a two-seater. No room for the bag of toys or a co-pilot. He's a big guy, he takes up a lot of space."

She laughed into her coffee. Maybe it was the head injury, or the amnesia but it was kind of cute how he talked about this stuff as if it were real. "Well, the town council refuses to give us any money to update things and the shop owners can no longer afford to keep it up on their own. And our mayor doesn't care anymore. So Santa's Bluetooth will have to wait."

The little house with its fake snow roof was padlocked so they could only peer through the dusty windows at the empty little room. Tools lay forgotten on the floor, a few patio tables and chairs were stacked in a corner. All forgotten relics from another day.

"This?" he asked, hands still cupped to frame his face as he peeked inside. "This is supposed to inspire kids to believe?"

Her cheeks went warm. It was hard to look at these things through the eyes of an outsider. "Well, once it would have held a big chair and someone to play Santa, maybe some elves. Years ago we even had some reindeer on loan from a petting zoo. But now…"

"I get it." He pulled away from the window. "No one comes anymore so you can't afford to make it nicer, but since it's not nice, nobody comes."

She took another sip of her latte, noticing it had gone lukewarm. "Something like that." The cold from the sidewalk had begun to seep through the slipper sock and the breeze that hadn't seemed so nippy while under the awning swirled around her like an embrace from Jack Frost himself. Funny, now he had her doing it, acting like this stuff was real.

She hugged her arms to her sides while he scrutinized the entire structure, even climbing up on a railing to get a better look at the roof. "It's awful," he said when he returned from his investigation. "No wonder today's kids don't believe."

"Or maybe they'd rather believe in online gaming and virtual reality instead of some antiquated world that doesn't exist." She winced at the bitter edge to her voice. She still remembered how it had felt to realize none of it existed, not even here in Christmasville.

"Ouch." He shrugged out of his coat and draped it over her shoulders, the warmth of his body heat and the smell of chocolate chip cookies surrounded her. Oh, why did he have to be a gentleman, that made it even harder not to fall for him.

She paused for a moment, closing her eyes to savor the cookie aroma, the sudden sensation of joy and happy memories that flooded her. Christmas morning when her parents were still alive, a puppy under the tree, a soft, pink baby doll, books, a shiny new pink bicycle and—

"You okay?"

She opened her eyes, feeling a bit silly. "Uh yeah. Sorry." She hugged the lapels of the jacket closer as they fell into step once again. "Aren't you cold?"

"Me? No. This weather is nothing. It feels good. Besides—" He tugged at the sweater. "This is acrylic so it's like being wrapped in plastic. We sell these, too, but only in wool or cashmere."

"We? That sounds like a memory."

He blinked. "Yeah. You're right. It was there just a second ago but…poof." He gestured into the air. "It's gone now."

"Well, it's a start." She continued to sip her now-cool latte as they walked back toward the shop. It was good he was beginning to remember things, but if she wasn't careful, she'd get too used to him being around.

****

Back in the shop, Lucy headed to the basement to pull out some inventory boxes. Jake breathed a sigh of relief—now he would have a chance to re-assemble the mechanical elves.

Since time was short, he took out the pocket watch and made a fervent wish for them to return to their original condition. In less time than it took to blink, the animated characters were reassembled. There wasn't time to check the gauge on the watch to see how much magic he had used; he could hear Lucy moving things around below.

He hurried to the door that led to the storeroom and met her coming up the stairs carrying a cardboard box. "I can do it," she protested as he took the box form her.

"Please don't tell me you are one of those women who won't give guys a chance to be chivalrous."

Her cheeks flushed a rosy pink. "No, I'm just used

to doing things for myself."

"And you're afraid if you let someone help you might actually like it," he said after setting the box on the counter near the cash register.

"Maybe but—wow, how did you put them back together so fast?" She rushed over to where the animated figures stood upright on the floor. She fingered the material of one of the sweaters. "They look almost brand new. Jake, this is incredible. I didn't realize you cleaned them and touched up the paint, too."

He hadn't realized it, either. No wonder the watch in his pocket felt so warm against his thigh, it was working overtime. "Um… Yeah. I mean I had the time, so why not?" He gave a nervous laugh. "But the motor— it needs to be cleaned now and then. The dust gets into the gears and gums up the oil. It makes it harder for them to run." He lifted the first one and climbed onto the ledge inside the front window.

"I didn't know that." She lifted the second one and handed it to him, watching as he plugged them in. They began to move with an enthusiasm he'd bet they hadn't shown in years.

"Come to think of it, I remember now—my grandfather used to pull them apart and clean them every year."

"Now you know why."

He climbed down from the front window and put his hands on his hips. "This must be a lot on you. Taking all of this over by yourself."

She raised her brows and looked away. "It is what it is."

He frowned. Why was she so reluctant to talk about it? "I'm sorry. None of my business."

She turned and headed to the box he'd left on the counter. "Well, I have some inventory to unpack. What are your plans for today? Are you…"

"Are you asking me to leave?"

"What? No." She whirled to face him. "I just wasn't sure if…."

"I have no plans, at least until I figure things out. Why don't I stick around and help you today? I mean, it's kind of my fault you have that bum foot."

"It's fine."

"I'm guessing you wouldn't admit if it wasn't. I noticed you limping on the way back from our walk." He walked over to the box and lifted it. "Why don't you get off that foot and I'll unpack the box, I'd like to learn more about what you sell."

"You don't have to—"

"Sit."

She opened her mouth as if to protest but he held tight to the box, holding it out of her reach, until she sat.

He tore open the box and peered inside. The smell of plastic nearly overwhelmed him. Cheap looking doodads and ornaments. He held up a hollow Christmas ball with the hanger attached haphazardly. "Really?"

She shook her head. "I'll send that one back."

"Luce, why are you selling this stuff? It looks like it came from one of those dollar places."

"I don't have a choice. Revenue is down so I can't afford to buy decent inventory."

"And cheap inventory means not much income." He let out a deep sigh. "I get it."

"Yes. Right now online sales are the only things keeping the store going, that and the hand-painted ornaments I sell on eBay and Etsy."

Was it really that bad down here? No wonder these people were all so unhappy and belief in Santa was nonexistent. "Why don't you sell hand-painted ornaments here in the store?"

"I do." She gestured toward a display case off to one side. "But I don't get nearly as much traffic in the store as I do online. In fact, I'm probably—"

The bell over the door jingled and the coffee shop guy poked his head in. "We still on for tonight? Seven o'clock at the coffee shop?"

She nodded. "I'll be there."

Coffee Guy frowned in his direction. "Why are you still here?"

"It's fine, Rick," Lucy said. "Jake is helping me out."

Before closing the door again, the guy gestured to indicate he would be keeping an eye on him. "Just be careful, Luce."

A twinge of annoyance nagged at him, followed by something else he wasn't sure how to define. Were they dating? "Isn't he a little old for you?"

"What?" Her startled gaze flew to the window. "Eeew. No, he's like—my dad's age, if he had lived, anyway. It's a meeting for all the merchants in town." She pulled in a sharp breath. "A developer has made us an offer and I think we're going to take it."

Chapter Seven

The blinds in the coffee shop were closed, only a dim glow could be seen inside. Lucy tapped at the door and Barbara peeked out before opening it.

A jingle of bracelets and a whiff of perfume met her as she was enfolded in a warm hug. "How you doin' baby?" The older woman asked. She pulled back, still holding Lucy's shoulders. "I've been worried about you."

"I'm okay, just a sprained ankle." She directed a thumb over her shoulder. "This is Jake."

"Mm-hmmmm." The woman's disapproval was evident. "We all heard about *him*."

"I—that was a misunderstanding."

Lucy pulled off her scarf and jacket and hung them on a hook. Jake did the same and strolled across the room toward an empty table. Dim after hours lighting, and clear holiday lights lent a soft glow to the interior of the coffee shop. The dark wood furnishings and a brick fireplace gave it a cozy feel. Madison sat at a small table off to one side, surrounded by books, head bent over her laptop, working on homework.

Lucy took a quick inventory of the assembled merchants, many of whom she'd known most of her life and considered family. Barbara, of course, who owned the diner; Tim and Brad who owned another shop; the Kims, a married couple who ran the lodge; Laura, the town historian; and Pam and her sister Sarita who ran a home bakery that supplied vegan treats to shops around the area.

Others were newer to Christmasville, and she suspected, more eager to cut their losses and sell out than the rest of them. But things had gotten rough enough in recent years that even long-time merchants were talking about pulling up stakes and leaving.

Her friend Brad patted an empty seat near him and his partner Tim as she approached. They were among the newer merchants, and owned a sporting goods store up the street from her. They rented everything from snowshoes to bicycles for tourists and scheduled shuttle tours.

Brad stood to air kiss both of her cheeks. "Hello, beautiful."

A warm flush came over her and she laughed. "You know coming from a straight guy that would sound creepy, but not from you."

He chuckled and nodded behind him where Jake stood looking a bit awkward. "He's cute."

"Is he?" Lucy asked with a laugh. "I hadn't noticed."

"You doing okay?" Tim asked, leaning across the table. "I know this is rough."

The lump in her throat grew ten sizes and her eyes stung with tears. "It is. For all of us, I think."

Everyone seated at the table nodded.

Rick moved to the door and opened it to let Barbara's daughter Frieda, a real estate lawyer, inside. After closing and locking the door, he switched off the outside lights. "Can I get anyone coffee?"

"You wait on people all day," Lucy said, starting to rise. "Why don't you let me get it?"

A hand on her shoulder stilled her. "You stay off that foot," Tim said. "I'll get the coffee. Who wants regular and who wants decaf?" He took a count before heading behind the counter and the group at the table settled in to talk.

As the conversation around her faded, Lucy studied Jake. He stood, hands clasped behind his back as he studied the framed black and white photos on the walls. Pictures of the town from its heyday when Christmasville had been the place to go for year-round Christmas. He turned and met her gaze, and her heart did a ridiculous somersault.

"So," Rick began once the coffee had been served. "What's the latest offer and where do we stand?"

Frieda pulled a folder from her briefcase. "Well, the donut place is being very generous, they really like this location. But the other place is willing to beat their offer. They think their whole coffee bar/bookstore vibe is well suited to this location."

"It's a prime location," Brad said. "Right here on the corner in the center of town, it's perfect."

Several nods went around the table.

"But wouldn't they need a lot more space?" Lucy asked. "Those bookstores are huge."

"That's where it gets interesting," Frieda said. "They want the businesses alongside it, too, as well as the ones behind for a parking lot."

Jake turned to look over his shoulder, frowning.

"Where does that leave the rest of us?" Barbara asked.

"Screwed." Mr. Kim, who owned the Reindeer Lodge scowled. "Once those businesses go, the rest of us will go bankrupt in no time."

More nods.

"Barb, who is going to come eat in your diner if there are no more tourists? Who is going to ride the tourist shuttle?" Mr. Kim slammed one fist on the table. "Who is going to stay at my damn lodge if the half the town is taken over by some giant chain bookstore?"

"Look," Rick turned his hands palms up on the table. "This was mine and Janine's dream. Together. But it was never my dream to do this alone. She's gone now and I have a sixteen-year-old who can't sleep past four a.m. on school days because she has to come here with me to open the store. I'm putting in eighteen-hour days and just scraping by. I can't even afford to hire part time help this year. I can't do it anymore." His voice cracked and he pulled in a deep breath. "Madi is off to college in a couple years. If I take their offer, I can pay off the medical bills left from Janine, pay for college—give my kid an actual life again."

Barbara reached over to place her hand on Rick's. "I know, baby, I know."

"I don't mind being here, Daddy," Madison spoke up. "It's not so bad getting up early."

Rick's eyes misted over, and he cast a glance toward his daughter. "You see what a great kid I raised?"

Lucy sent a smile his way.

Frieda pulled another folder from her briefcase. "Rick has a good point and for the rest of you wondering how your businesses would be impacted…" She flipped open the folder and removed a sheet of paper, turning it so those at the table could see. "A major retail chain is considering the other side of the block for their new super center. This is their offer." She tapped a red fingernail next to a number with a whole lot of zeroes.

"It would be divided among all of you with businesses on the other side of the street."

Lucy couldn't tear her gaze away from the paper in front of her. Even shared among her business neighbors, it was more money than she could dream of. For a moment, thoughts of what she could do ran through her mind. She wouldn't have to worry about paying the bills month to month. And she could travel. She hadn't set foot outside of New York State since her parents had died.

She looked up to meet Brad's gaze across the table. He nodded toward the number on the page, and she suspected he was thinking along the same lines.

"You should take it, Luce," Tim looked from the paper up to her. "You promised your grandmother you wouldn't let yourself get stuck here. You're young, you could finally enjoy your life."

Brad nodded. "And we could retire and move someplace warm. No more northern New York winters."

"Hold on now," Barbara cautioned. "Don't try to talk Lucy into it just to make it easier on yourselves to take the offer without feeling guilty. We all need to think long and hard about this."

"I say it's all or none—either we all take it, or none of us do," Mr. Kim said. "That's the only way to be fair."

"You just want to hold out and force us all to stay," Brad said. "Nice for you but what about the rest of us trying to keep our heads above water?"

"He didn't say that," Rick raised his voice above the arguing. "But he makes a good point. If one of us goes, it hurts the others. We should present a unified front."

"Wait." Lucy put her fingertips to her temples. She could hardly think straight for all the chatter around her, not to mention the thoughts ricocheting back and forth in her mind. "Frieda, how long do we have to think about this?"

"Not long," the woman answered. "Thanksgiving is week after next so that will buy us a few extra days. But they want an answer soon, and they won't hesitate to start lowering their price if we take too long to respond."

****

The walk back to Lucy's place was silent. Jake strolled alongside her, keeping his steps slow due to her bad foot, content to take cues from her on whether or not to talk about what had just happened.

The town was quiet, the shops closed up and dark this time of night. They reached Lucy's store and she paused to look at the door. Her shoulders sagged. "I think I'd like to walk a bit more, clear my head."

"Mind if I tag along?" he asked.

She looked up at him and rolled her eyes. "Don't tell me you're being chivalrous again."

"Maybe a little." He shrugged. "And maybe I think you could use the company."

"Suit yourself." She continued down the sidewalk.

"And I saw you slip that pepper spray in your pocket yesterday, I know you aren't defenseless."

A laugh escaped her. "Oh, you saw that, did you?"

He nodded. "I don't blame you, but I promise I'm not like that. I'm too busy trying to figure out why I'm here to think about attacking you."

"Lucky for me, then." She tucked her hands into her pockets as a cold breeze wafted over them. "I'd think you'd be more interested in figuring out who you are."

"That, too," he admitted. *In more ways than one.*

"Weird how neither one of us has a working cell

phone," she said. "I need to get mine fixed and you didn't have one on you. So I can't help you figure out things."

They didn't use cell phones at the North Pole, instead they had the ETS and snow globe technology. "Yeah, I must have…forgotten it."

She laughed. "You really must have been out of it. Who forgets their phone these days?"

He looked at her and laughed. For a split second he held her dark brown gaze. Something magnetic moved between them, and she dragged her eyes away.

The appreciation he'd noted in her expression sent a surge of heat through him. He was used to female attention, but at the North Pole he was an exotic element—the only guy who happened to be more than five feet tall.

"The park is just ahead," she said, taking a hand from her jacket to point to the other side of the street. "It's actually the other side of the park from where we were today at the Santa house."

They crossed the deserted main street and headed for the grassy expanse. "This is where the parade used to begin. "

"Parade?" he asked, frowning.

"The one from the photos. I saw you looking at them in the coffee shop. You seemed pretty interested."

"Oh, that. Yeah." He'd been interested all right, one photo in particular. A familiar elf in the crowd with curly hair sticking out from under her hat.

"Those photos have always fascinated me," she went on. "The men in their hats with cigarettes in their hands, the women in dresses and high heels—and it was probably cold, yet they look so happy. People don't dress up like that anymore."

She turned and trudged up a small incline toward a gazebo. She stopped to gaze up at it, before stepping inside to run her hand over a low bench almost reverently. "I used to love coming here to sit when I was a kid. I'd sneak out after my grandparents had gone to bed and just sit here and read a book, or watch the stars."

Even in the dark he could see that the paint, much like the rest of Christmasville, was chipped and weather worn.

"It used to be lit with clear lights all year round; it was beautiful. More than once I fell asleep right here on this bench and had to hurry back home before my grandparents noticed I was gone and worried."

An idea came to him, and he slipped his hand in the pocket of his jeans. Yep. The pocket watch was there. "Where did the lights plug in?"

"Oh, it hasn't been lit in years, I'm sure they no longer work."

"You never know. But I wish I could see it all lit up." At those words, the watch in his pocket grew warm and vibrated. He stepped outside of the gazebo and went around to one side where an outlet appeared, so new and shiny it almost glowed in the dark. A cord dangled nearby, and he reached for it to connect the two.

In an instant, the little gazebo glowed against the night sky.

Lucy gasped in pleasure. "I can't believe they still work, last I knew the town had taken down all the decorations around the park."

"Well looks like they missed these," he said, stepping back inside.

She laughed and sat on the bench, gazing up at the lights. "It's silly, isn't it? How something so simple can seem so magical?"

He studied her for long moments. The joy in her face tugged at something deep inside him. For once he wasn't thinking about getting a girl into bed, only about making her smile. What the hell was wrong with him?

He took a seat beside her on the bench. She released a deep breath. "I really don't know what to do. It's such a big change and there's so much to think about."

He picked up the hand that rested on her lap. She looked at him as if startled at the contact but didn't pull away.

"The thing is, I may not even get to decide for myself. Mr. Kim is right. We all have to be on board with the decision, so I'll have to go with what everyone else decides."

Personally, Jake didn't see any of them being on the same page about it anytime soon. But he held his tongue, she didn't need that worry right now.

"I've never dared let myself dream about a different life. And now… it's kind of scary to think it could happen whether I want it to or not."

Well that was something he could relate to. "Change is scary. Sticking with what's familiar is a hell of a lot easier."

She gave a soft laugh. "Your life has certainly been changed and it probably wasn't your choice."

The memory of how angry his mother had been the other morning teased his brain. "No, it wasn't." He looked over at the girl beside him. "But it hasn't been all bad."

Her cheeks flushed a delicate pink, and she returned her gaze to the twinkle lights. "It's just hard to imagine something different."

Maybe he could help. He reached an arm to wrap it around her shoulders.

"What are you doing?" she asked.

"I'm not making a move," he said, "just keeping you warm."

Her body relaxed against his and she sighed. "Why do you always smell like chocolate chip cookies?"

"Like what?" he teased. "I think that's all in your head."

"Maybe. But I like it." She went silent for several seconds. "I'm glad they put the twinkle lights back up, even if they didn't tell anyone. I wish they would bring back the town tree."

"Where did it go?" He gazed up at the lights, reminded briefly of the lights at home in the North Pole.

"There was a Christmas tree farm just outside of town that donated a tree to the town every year. They went out of business, so we don't have a town tree anymore. It used to be a big deal." She sighed and her head dropped toward his shoulder. "The merchants would collect toy and food donations and we'd hand them out at the tree lighting." She yawned. "Some of us would leave baskets of food and toys on people's front steps the week of Christmas, too."

"Are there a lot of needy folks around Christmasville?"

"Outside of town, yes. Factories have closed, manufacturing plants shut down. There are a lot of people out of work. This will be the first year the merchants can't afford to give them a Christmas."

Kids without toys at Christmas time? "Not on my watch."

Chapter Eight

The blue-white glow of the snow globe lit the storage room below the store. So far, Merry had not responded to his messages but Jake persisted, repeatedly signaling until at last, her sleep-weary face appeared.

"Dash, do you have any idea what time—"

"Don't call me that."

She rolled her eyes. "Did you call me to argue about your elf name?"

"No. I want to know what's going on. I can always tell when you're up to something."

"What is this about?" She yawned. "I only just got to sleep."

"Why did you send me here?"

"Honey, I told you, it was time you experienced life in the—"

"I saw you. In the pictures from the old days. Holding a little boy. Me, I assume."

After a beat of silence, followed by a flash, his mother stood before him in her robe and slippers in one blinding instant.

"Thought that might get your attention," he said, adding a tinge of smug to his tone. Folding both arms over his chest, Jake regarded his mother with a smirk. "What's up with this town? You sent me here for a reason."

Merry shook her head. "Nothing that I can think of.

I guess maybe when I sent you, I was thinking of the time we were here."

"We? You mean the two of us?"

She sighed and turned a slow circle. "Is there some place to sit?"

"Don't change the subject."

With a roll of her eyes and a wave of her hand, a comfortable looking, over-stuffed armchair appeared. She sank into it, running a hand over her face. "Peppering me with questions after barely an hour of sleep…"

He checked his watch. Four a.m. here meant it was midnight at the North Pole.

"What pictures are you going on about?" she muttered into one hand.

"Hanging on the wall in the coffee shop across the street. Lots of them, from the town's heyday. And their Christmas parade."

For a split second, she paled.

"There's a picture of a woman—you—in the crowd holding a baby, maybe two or three years old. Why were we here?"

She stifled a yawn and waved a dismissive hand. "Nick used to come here to play Santa in their parade. He loved the town's Christmas spirit. I came along one year to help. Single mothers don't have much choice but to bring their kids along." She blinked and a mug appeared in her hands, steam rising from the top. He recognized the tag on the string that dangled over the cup as her favorite brand of chamomile.

"So that's all it was?"

"Yes, I thought you'd enjoy it. And you did. You had a wonderful time."

He leaned a hip against a shelving unit attached to the wall. "So why did Nick stop coming?"

Merry looked thoughtful. "The town lost its spirit. There weren't as many believers. He got discouraged. We all did."

"This place is dying, you know. The merchants plan to sell out to some major developer."

Her eyes grew wide. "Oh, that's such a shame."

Jake nodded. "It gets worse. Apparently for a long time now the merchants have collected food and toys for underprivileged families. Things here are so bad they can't do it anymore."

She shook her head in empathy.

"Mom, we're talking about kids without toys. At Christmas." He paced the length of the room. "Did you send me here on purpose? You can't expect me to fix this, I don't have any magic." He reached the far wall and pivoted. "And even if I did find a way to make it better this year, what happens when I leave?"

"Nick would never let kids go without toys at Christmas, you know that."

"Did you ever think maybe the two go hand-in-hand—Nick stopped coming here because there weren't as many believers. Maybe they felt that loss—the magic that he brought wasn't there anymore."

"No, I never thought about it. I'll look into it and see if we can find a way to send the town a little Christmas magic. Maybe it will help for a while."

"And don't take it out of whatever magic you put in the watch, I've already used too much."

"You need to be careful with that, Dash. If you use it all, you won't be able to get home."

Jake's stomach bottomed out. "Wait? You tell me

that *now*?" Memories of how indiscriminately he'd been using that magic came to taunt him.

Footsteps sounded overhead. With a fast glance for the ceiling, he realized Lucy must be awake. Crap.

With a flash and whiff of cinnamon and vanilla, Merry—and the chair—were gone.

"Jake?" Lucy called from the stairs. "Are you down there?"

"Uh…yeah." Shoot, how was he going to explain why he was in the basement? "I umm…" A box appeared in his arms, complete with a thick coating of dust. He frowned but decided to go with it and stepped closer. "I couldn't sleep so I thought I'd put out some more inventory. I found this."

"What is it?"

He shrugged and headed up the stairs. "I don't know, let's find out."

He carried the box into the middle of the room and set it down. Lucy regarded it, frowning. "I've never seen that down there."

"It was uh…behind the furnace."

"Funny, I cleaned back there a few weeks ago. I don't remember a box." She dropped to her knees, running her fingers over the word "ornaments" scrawled in pen. "That's my grandfather's handwriting."

"Well, let's see what's inside."

She tugged open the box and took out a handwritten packing slip. "This company went out of business years ago."

She set it aside and opened the flaps with a gasp of surprise. Inside were hundreds of glass ornaments, all from another era. Vintage by today's standards, but brand new when they had been put away. "These are beautiful." She lifted one gold ornament with the words Merry Christmas written in silver and gold glitter. "I can't believe these have been down there all this time." She dug into the box once more and this time pulled up an ornament with a tiny angel atop complete with feathery wings.

She stared at him with wide brown eyes. "People love this sort of thing, they always come in here looking for vintage ornaments like this." She set it aside and sat back on her knees.

Nice one, Merry. "So you can sell these?"

She shrugged. "I suppose, but more importantly, I think I can recreate them. "

"You can?"

"Yes, but with modern materials that won't break or fade as easily. Vintage look but with modern durability. I think they would sell really well, both online and in the store." A sparkle lit her eyes. "This might be just the thing I need to rebrand my store."

****

Later that evening, Lucy decided to give Jake a tour of the area outside Christmasville town limits. It also gave her a chance to replace her cell phone since the old one was ruined beyond repair.

They stopped at a popular chain restaurant for a dinner of burgers and shakes, Jake's treat since Lucy had bought breakfast. On the way back she took the long way, showing him different sites outside of town.

At one traffic light, she pointed to a church, the steeple lit by a single bulb. "That's where my grandparents and my parents were both married. It's closed now."

They drove on a bit farther and she pointed out the

fire house, town hall and library.

She turned a corner and drove about ten minutes until they came to an old white farmhouse that stood dark and still. A chain link fence went around the property. "This is the Christmas tree farm that went under."

She pulled into the driveway and pointed toward a row of trees, barely visible against the night sky. "See all the trees back there? Those are the oldest, the ones that would have been ready this year. I guess they will just keep growing now until some developer buys the lot and cuts them down to put a drugstore or fast-food restaurant there." Her voice broke. "I used to help out here seasonally when I was in high school; I went to school with their granddaughters."

"Want to get out and take a look around?" he offered, curious to see what was left of the place.

She shrugged. "If you want."

They exited the car and walked down the drive until they came to the fence. Lucy curled her fingers around the mesh and peered inside. "It's a shame. They could have let people come and cut down a tree, at least made use of them for a season. It's not like anyone is going to use them." She reached down to finger the padlock and chain. "The shop owners all bought a fresh tree every year; the fragrance really put people in the spirit and a lot of times, tourists stopped here before driving home and bought a wreath or some pine garland."

She looked up at him, her brown eyes full of anguish. "It's so hard to watch it all die like this, I'm glad my grandparents aren't here to see it."

He reached down to touch the lock. "I wish there was a way to get inside," he said, making sure to enunciate each word clearly. The watch in his pocket grew warm and when he reached to touch the lock, it fell open. "Well look at that. Someone forgot to lock up." He eased the chain away and pushed the gate open.

"Jake, what are you doing?"

"Aren't you curious about what's left?" He reached for her hand. She hesitated, looking behind her as though expecting sirens to start wailing. "Come on."

Shyly, hesitantly, she reached for his hand, and he helped her through. Some weird feeling slammed him hard in the gut as her fingers curled around his. What was up with that? He never really held hands with girls, the touch was too innocent, too sweet. Why waste time when the end goal was getting naked and horizontal?

But with Lucy…there was something intimate about the feel of her warm, soft hand in his that brought out some strange alpha male protective instinct. Like if an angry bear suddenly ran out from behind the trees, he'd fight it off— or at least help her climb to safety. He shook off the notion. Merry would be shocked at him having such noble thoughts.

Once she was safely on the other side of the fence he made no effort to release her hand. She didn't seem to mind.

They trudged forward, their steps made awkward by ruts in the dirt from years of trucks and other farm equipment. Up ahead was a barn, the red color faded to a brownish hue. A weathered sign in white script read "Christmasville Tree Farm and Event Center."

Lucy reached to trace her fingers over the peeling letters. "This was a venue for large parties, big dinners, wedding receptions—all kinds of things. I worked some of the events and a lot of weekends during busy season to help out."

The doors were padlocked so they moved on, walking until they came to a large greenhouse. There was no lock here, so Jake opened the door and they stepped inside. The building still held a bit of warmth from the sunlight earlier in the day.

"Cozy," he said, mostly to break the silence since she hadn't said anything for a while.

"Yeah." Her voice came out a little strangled. "It looks so… empty."

"What did it used to look like?"

"Trees," she laughed. "Everywhere. Row after row of little seedlings and saplings. They stayed here in the nursery until they were big enough—and the outdoors was warm enough—for them to be safely planted." She turned a half circle, making no attempt to let go of his hand. "Oh!"

She let go this time and rushed to where an overturned table lay on the floor. She knelt beside it where a pile of dirt had spilled, and the dried, brown remains of several young trees remained. "I can't believe they left them here to die like that."

He waited, uncertain what to say until she swiped at her cheeks and a sniffle carried to him. "Luce?" Something told him this was about more than dead trees.

"I…" she shook her head. "I must seem like a crazy person, crying over dead plants." She rose to her feet, one brittle tree in her hand. "But this feels like…like it represents what's happened to Christmasville. Dried up. Dead. No one to care."

A relieved sigh escaped him. So she wasn't upset about the plants. Followed by a slight sense of panic. He had no idea how to handle a weepy female. When Merry got bitchy or the Frost twins got teary-eyed and clingy, he gave them space for a good seven to fourteen days until the storm passed.

But this wasn't hormones, this was a woman watching her world end. Instinct took over and he crossed the short distance between them to pull her into his arms. The dam burst and she pressed her face into his chest, sobbing in earnest, her body racked with emotion.

He had no idea how long they stood there, five minutes, maybe ten, him holding her tight, rubbing her back, offering soothing words, until she grew quiet.

"I'm so glad my grandparents aren't here to see what's happened to this town," she murmured.

A gust of cool air rushed past his feet, bringing a whiff of cinnamon and vanilla. Oh hell, what was *she* up to?

Lucy raised her head from this chest to look up into his face. "Is it just me or—"

Not knowing how else to distract her, he did the only thing he could think of. He kissed her.

He meant it to be tender, comforting. But the sweet smell of her—baby powder and honeysuckle—filled his nostrils. The taste of her—warm and comforting, like hot cocoa on a cold night, overwhelmed him.

Her arms went around his neck, and he forgot that Merry was somewhere nearby, didn't care anymore what she was up to or why she'd sent elf magic their way. He fisted a hand into Lucy's hair—cool silken strands wove between his fingers. He moaned as her lips parted beneath his, granting him entry.

He slid a hand purposefully down her spine, fighting the urge to continue the journey down her backside and haul her up against his raging erection. Somehow, not doing that, and not allowing his hands or his mind to wander to other places, was hotter, the sensation more intense than he'd have guessed.

When at last she pulled back, her face held a dazed look that mimicked the sensations raging through him. "What was that about?"

He shrugged. "I don't know. I guess it just felt like the right time."

"Did you happen to smell—" she looked down at the tree still clutched in her hand and gave a little gasp. "Do you see that? It still has some green on it. I didn't notice that before."

He let out a relieved sigh. So that was what Merry was up to, rejuvenating a dead plant. Did that mean the intense feelings when kissing Lucy were real, not some magic created by his mother?

"Why don't you take it home and put it in a pot," he suggested. "Then someday when you settle somewhere else, maybe you can plant it outside. A piece of home."

She nodded. "I like that idea."

****

The ride back to town was quiet. Lucy concentrated on the dark road ahead, confused by the jittery sensations fluttering in her stomach.

She'd been attracted to him from the start, but there was a lot to be considered before diving headlong into a fling with a guy who didn't even remember who he was.

The kiss had been a surprise, not simply because it was unexpected but because of how amazing it had been. She definitely wanted more. She slid a glance over at him across the bench seat.

He leaned one arm against the door, thumb on his chin, deep in thought. The black leather jacket accented his dark hair and brows. Headlights from a passing vehicle lit his face and she got another look at those baby blue eyes …her stomach did that little flip flop thing. She forced her gaze back to the road. Geez, what was she, twelve?

It had been a long time since she'd felt anything like this—college exactly. Daniel, her college boyfriend, lived in Syracuse, a little more than two hours south. The distance was just too much once she had left school to move in full time with Gran. Not to mention Daniel's life had consisted of school and parties while hers was about caregiving, driving Gran to chemo and doctor appointments, running the store. And worrying.

Her life had become a series of grown-up concerns that most twenty-two-year-olds couldn't relate to. Daniel had been no exception. After a while, she had broken things off out of fairness to him. He had protested, but she'd sensed relief in his voice.

Jake shifted to look at her.

She glanced over at him again. "It's not much farther, we're almost there." She peeked at the little tree on the seat between them. She'd packed some dirt around it and put it in a pot, but didn't want to add water until it was indoors in the warmth.

Something weird had happened back there and it wasn't just the kiss. She'd smelled cookies. Not the usual chocolate chip scent she associated with Jake, either. It had smelled like…Christmas.

And for a second—just one split second—she'd felt a sense of magic, that same feeling in the air that only little kids could feel. The one that sort of grew out of you when you stopped believing.

There had not been a smidge of green on that little tree before that moment. And then, after he kissed her…

She shook her head. Where was she going with this? Intent on distracting her thoughts, she reached for the radio. "How about some music?"

She turned the knob and a familiar seasonal song by Alvin and the Chipmunks filled the cab. She rolled her eyes and reached for the dial.

The warmth of his hand covered hers. "I like that song."

Heat filtered through her insides at the contact. What was it about him—hot guy yet almost childlike in his love for all things Christmas?

It would be interesting to know his story, if he ever remembered. But did she even want to know the truth?

That thought was still in her mind when she turned down Main Street. Her gaze immediately went to a very tall object covered in colorful lights.

Jake sat up straighter. "What the…"

"It's a Christmas tree." She said it as much to herself as to him. She pulled the truck over and switched on the four ways. A crowd of people had formed around the sight, pointing, laughing, and smiling.

"That wasn't there when we left." She checked for oncoming traffic and climbed out the driver's side door, careful not to put weight on her bad foot.

Barbara waved her over, a smile lighting her face. "Isn't it magnificent?"

"Who did this?" Lucy looked around, waving a quick hello to many of her fellow merchants.

"Nobody knows."

Lucy approached the tree, fingering the branches, amazed to find it was a live tree. How on earth did someone drive that into town and set it up without anyone seeing? "It's right where we always had our town tree," she marveled. "So whoever put it here knows…"

Beside her, Jake shrugged. "Or maybe it's just the center of town and a good spot for a tree?"

"And nobody saw anything?"

Rick stepped forward, his hands tucked into the pockets of his jacket. "Nope. The lights went out—all of Main Street went dark for about thirty seconds. And when they came back on—there it was."

"We didn't see or hear anything," Madison piped up from behind him. "But then we saw the Christmas lights and were like—what is *that*?"

"Out of nowhere," Brad said, coming to stand beside her. "Isn't it beautiful?"

She nodded. "But the tree farm went under last year, so who donated it? And… How?"

Barbara grabbed her hand, squeezing it. "You know, baby girl, I don't even care. Whoever did it gave this town some joy and I'm just so grateful."

Lucy stared up at the tree. Her friend was right, she should focus on that instead of wondering at the insanity of it all.

Madison began to sing "Oh, Christmas tree…" and within seconds everyone chimed in.

Jake's deep voice mingled with the others as they sang. Lucy closed her eyes as he slipped an arm around her shoulders, and she inhaled the smell of chocolate chip cookies, mingled with the aroma she'd noticed in the greenhouse—cinnamon and vanilla.

She opened her eyes and looked around but the only other person who seemed to notice the fragrance was Rick—his nose twitched, and he looked around, as though expecting someone to be there.

He met her gaze and gave her a bright smile. She

hadn't seen her friend this relaxed and happy in a long time. In fact, the faces on all her business neighbors as they sang Christmas carols and gazed up at the tree were full of joy and wonder.

Odd. First a box of vintage Christmas ornaments turned up in a basement she'd cleaned many times yet never uncovered. Then, a little Christmas tree came back to life. Now a huge fully decorated Christmas tree had appeared in the center of town with no explanation.

Funny, she'd never thought about it before. But weird things had been happening ever since Jake showed up in town.

Chapter Nine

After a restless night, Lucy rose before dawn. The memory of kissing Jake brought up all kinds of feelings she'd long since buried, but it was more than that.

Instead, she'd tossed and turned, reminded once more about how much she loved this town and her fellow merchants. How they'd rallied around her when her grandmother had passed, and then around Rick when he lost his wife.

Standing out in the cold last night in that impromptu caroling session had brought back the sense of family and belonging she'd always known here.

So rather than sleep she'd spent the night wondering *what if*—both about Jake and her business.

Daylight had yet to appear when she finally put her feet to the floor, slid into her slippers and padded into the kitchen. She'd just popped a pod in the coffee machine when a pounding came on the door downstairs.

She glanced at the clock on the wall. A little past five a.m. Only one person she knew would be out and about at this hour. She hurried to the living room window and peeked around the blinds. A soft, powdery coating of snow blanketed the ground, but other than that she saw nothing out of the ordinary.

"Luce!" Below, Rick waved an arm to get her attention. "You have to come see this!"

She frowned but grabbed her robe and hurried down

the stairs.

Jake met her as she unlocked the door to step into the shop. "What's going on?"

She shrugged and rushed to the door, Jake at her heels.

As she unlocked the door, Rick frowned at the sight of Jake behind her. "Why are you still here?"

Lucy hugged her arms tighter to herself against the chill of the morning air. "What's going on?"

He stepped back, arms spread wide. "This."

"The snow? I mean it's pretty but…"

Rick took hold of her hand and tugged her out to the middle of the sidewalk. "Look." He pointed down the street.

She gazed in the direction he gestured. And gasped. All along the block, outside of each merchant's shop, were Christmas trees. Not giant trees like the one in the middle of town, but big enough to be seen from a distance. Ornaments and lights glowed all the way up and down Main Street.

"What the—who did this?" The cold seeped through her slippers into her feet, bringing a shiver. "Did you do this?"

Rick scoffed. "I couldn't afford to buy this many trees, let alone the decorations." He shrugged his shoulders. "And when would I find the time?"

She glanced over at Jake, who stood beside them. His hands were stuffed into the pockets of his jeans, shoulders hunched against the cold. His gaze moved from the view down the street back to Lucy. "So…do you guys always have weird stuff like this happening around here?"

****

By noon the local news stations had picked up on the story of the mysterious Christmas trees. By late afternoon, the national news channels were in town.

Jake avoided the cameras and the questions, happy to hear Lucy, Rick, and the other merchants tell their stories over and over.

Their excitement was infectious, and having the town in the news certainly wouldn't hurt. But he still couldn't figure out what Merry was up to.

Did she truly have a soft spot for this place simply because she'd spent a happy week or two here? Somehow it felt deeper than that.

Lucy came back inside the store after a joint interview with some of the other business owners in front of the town tree. Her cheeks and nose were flushed, her hair windblown but it was her radiant smile that tugged at his heart. She—and the other merchants—were enjoying the attention brought to their little town.

She unbuttoned her coat and hung it on a hook near the cash register. "You know, you should get out there and get your face on camera, maybe someone is looking for you."

A knot twisted in his chest. This amnesia charade was wearing a bit thin. He really wanted to tell her the truth, but how to begin? *I'm actually half elf and I live at the North Pole. My mother, a full-blooded elf made this happen. Santa Claus is like a dad to me, and Jack Frost and his wife are close family friends…*

Ehhh, maybe the amnesia thing was better after all.

Lucy regarded him with a smile. "What is that look?"

"Hmm?" He turned back to arranging the full-sized Santa on the sofa before the fireplace. He'd finally brought it out of storage for her. "Oh, just thinking, I guess."

"About?" She rubbed her hands together, huddling as though chilled and came toward him. "Santa looks good there, but where are you going to sleep?"

He shrugged. "I was thinking maybe I should get a room or something. I can't keep imposing on you. And it really seems to piss off your friend Rick."

"Oh, he's fine. He's sort of appointed himself my father figure over the years." She reached to tuck a throw pillow beneath Santa's head. "I think he's worried you'll take advantage of me. You know, seduce me or something."

The words hung heavy in the air between them. At last, Jake met her gaze and gave a half-hearted shrug. "Only if you want me to."

"What?" She shot a startled look at him.

"I'm teasing." He tossed the pillow at her. He certainly couldn't deny the electricity in the room. And maybe he was testing the waters a little just to see her reaction. She hadn't said no…

She straightened and tucked the blanket about Santa's body. "Maybe you getting a room somewhere is a good idea after all."

Or maybe she had…

Chapter Ten

The room at the Reindeer Lodge was cozy, decorated to give a log cabin feel, with twinkle lights over a rustic twig-look headboard, and a Christmas tree in one corner. Lots of plaid and plenty of fuzzy blankets and pillows with reindeer and snowmen themes.

Boy, they really took Christmas seriously around here. It almost made him a little homesick…

He'd just set his duffel bag on the bed and pulled out the snow globe when it glowed blue white.

But instead of the cinnamon and vanilla that signaled his mother, he got a whiff of peppermint. Uh oh. That meant…

Before he could complete the thought, he was being embraced by one of the Frost twins, her enthusiasm knocking him backward on the bed.

"Jakey!" she squealed, making no attempt to get up. Instead, she untangled herself, but straddled him on the bed. For a second he drank in the sight of someone from home. Especially a very blonde someone dressed in a snug white top that showed off her toned midriff and a red leather mini skirt. On either side of him were two very shapely legs and right above, practically heaving out of her shirt, two tantalizing breasts.

"Fauna, how did you find me?"

She gave him a playful slap. "I'm Flora."

Well, he'd had a fifty-fifty shot.

"I missed you, Jakey." Glossy cherry-red lips pouted. "You didn't tell us you were going away."

He pushed back with his elbows, attempting to sit up. "It uh, wasn't really planned."

She smoothed her hands over his chest. "I've been following your mom around for days, trying to figure it out. Then last night Fauna overheard her asking my dad to send some early snow to someplace called Christmasville." Her fingers continued down his chest to his stomach, pausing to tug at his belt.

He caught her hands. It wasn't that he didn't want to, it was just… wait a sec, why *didn't* he want to? Lucy. Her face came to mind, and he dropped his head back on the mattress in defeat. He was falling for her.

Flora climbed off him to stand near the bed, tugging her shirt over her head. The sight of her plentiful assets in that white lacy bra would have really revved his engine just a few days ago. "Flora, you can't stay."

"What?" Another pout. "Why not?"

"I uh…have to work. Tonight." Geez, even to his own ears it sounded like bull.

"Then let's have a quickie." She unzipped her skirt and began to shimmy it past her hips.

"No!" He winced at the harsh way that burst forth.

Flora regarded him with sad blue eyes and yet another practiced pout. "You don't think I'm pretty anymore."

"I—what? No. I mean…yes. You are, but…"

"But?" Tears shimmered in her eyes for a moment and then her face went deadly serious. "You've met someone else, haven't you?"

A whoosh of air rushed out of him, and he rose to his feet before she could straddle him again. "Maybe,

Faun, I don't know…"

"*Flo-ra*," she snarled.

Before he could answer a hesitant knock came at the door. "Jake?"

Holy crap. Speak of the devil.

Flora whirled toward the door. "Is that her?"

He caught hold of her arm. "You can't stay. Look, no one here knows about …people like us. There's been enough weird stuff going on without some hot elf chick being in my room."

"*Hot. Elf. Chick*?" She stamped her foot. "Is that all you think I am?" She grabbed her top from the bed and tugged it over her head. "I am *winter royalty*, remember? Jack Frost's daughter!"

"Okay, okay." He kept his voice soft, hoping she would do the same.

The knock came again. "Jake? Are you in there?"

Damn, she sounded upset.

"Can you just go?" he whispered. "I promise I'll talk to you later."

Flora/Fauna reached for the door. "I want to meet your new friend."

He yanked her back. "Fauna…"

"*Flora, Flora, Flora.*" She stamped her foot again and then a fiery glint came into her eyes. "Anyone ever tell you what happens when you piss off a snow princess?"

He closed his eyes and pinched the bridge of his nose. Why did he have a feeling he was about to find out?

A flash signaled her exit and he reached for the door. He had to have a good excuse for what took so long. He pulled the pocket watch out and wished he'd just taken a shower.

He yanked the door open in time to see Lucy turning to walk away. A chill rushed in from the hallway and he glanced down to see he was now soaking wet, clad only in a towel.

"Hey, sorry." A second towel was draped about his neck, so he lifted one end to wipe the water droplets from his face. "I was in the shower."

Her dark gaze scanned the length of him, and a tinge of pink flushed her cheeks. "I…thought I heard voices."

"TV was on."

"Oh."

He opened the door wider. "Come on in."

She gestured toward him. "Do you want to maybe put on some clothes first?"

No, quite the opposite in fact. But the sight of her damp cheeks and watery eyes caught his interest. "Luce, what's wrong?"

For a moment they were in a standoff, him standing there chilled by the cooler air from the hallway, her looking hesitant. "Why don't you come in, I'll get dressed."

She blinked. "Right. I'm sorry, you must be cold."

After closing the door behind her, he headed back into the bathroom. The pocket watch sat there on the sink, and he quickly made another wish for clean clothes.

A neatly folded stack of laundry appeared, and he grabbed them, sliding into the jeans and thick black sweater—thankfully without any flashing reindeer this time.

When he returned, he came up short. She held the snow globe in her hands, her face illuminated by the bluish-white glow. For a moment he wondered what she would see in it. He made a mental note to set it to Do Not

Disturb. And to leave it that way.

"Does it glow like that all the time?" she asked.

Only when my mother is spying on me. "No, it's just a light."

She tipped her head. "But it must have some special meaning for you. It was in your bag when you arrived, and you made a point to set it on the nightstand."

"I just didn't want it to get damaged." He held his breath as she continued to study it, worried someone else would burst forth.

"Well does it play music or something?" She turned it upside down. "Maybe if you looked at it, held it a while, it would jog your memory?"

"Luce, did you come here to talk about something?"

She set the snow globe back on the nightstand. "Yes."

He breathed a sigh of relief when it went dark.

"At an emergency meeting of the merchants tonight, we discussed this weird appearance of trees everywhere." She looked up at him with dark brown eyes full of emotion. "And…Frieda called. You know, Barbara's daughter, the real estate lawyer? With the renewed interest in the town the developers have increased their offer. A lot."

"And?"

She shook her head. "It went bad fast. Lots of arguing. You know how we said we all would go or none?"

He nodded, but her slumped shoulders and broken expression told him everything.

"Well, that's not the case anymore. Rick, Brad and Tim are done. They want out. Mr. Kim is furious. Pam and Sarita know it's the end for them, not being able to supply baked goods to the coffee shop." She pulled in a shaky breath. "It's over. The rest of us can't possibly stay afloat without the others."

He wanted to ask how she felt about that, but the answer was all over her face.

"I don't know if I'm relieved or devastated," she said. "I wasn't expecting this. Because of the news being here after the trees appeared, every hotel and bed and breakfast for thirty miles around is booked. I guess I got my hopes up that maybe…" She gazed at him with anguished brown eyes. "I didn't know who else to talk to."

"Any chance they'll change their minds?"

She shook her head. "I doubt it. It just doesn't make sense, why now when there is suddenly interest in the town again? Mr. Kim says the lodge is booked right through the New Year." She swiped at a tear. "I guess they realize that come mid-January, the town will all be forgotten again. Unless all these weird occurrences keep happening, Christmasville will fade back into oblivion. Maybe I'm being naïve, but I wish it would continue."

He closed his eyes. "I wish it would, too." In his pocket the watch grew warm, then hot against his thigh. Man, it was really working on something.

"I just wish I knew where it came from and how to keep it." She sniffed and looked up at him with watery eyes. "Is that so wrong?"

Her phone buzzed, and she pulled it from her jacket pocket. She glanced at the screen then shook her head. "It's Barbara. Toys and wrapped packages just appeared beneath all the trees." Her eyes widened to the size of frisbees. "Oh, my gosh. The presents are labeled—with the names of families from around town—the needy families I mentioned."

She frowned. "It's weird. Every time I tell you about something it happens. First the town Christmas tree, now the toys for the kids. Jake, do you have something to do with all of this?"

The temptation to tell her nearly overwhelmed him. He really wanted to. But not now, when she was emotionally spent. "Yeah, right." He forced a laugh. "Do you really think I could haul all of those trees around in the middle of the night? And how would I have gotten the town tree set up—we were together when it appeared."

"You're right, I know better." She placed her fingertips to her temples. "Forgive me for sounding so stupid. It's just…so many strange things have happened since you came to town."

He sat down beside her on the foot of the bed. "I can see where it would feel like that but it's just a coincidence, Lucy." He placed his hand over hers where it rested on her thigh. When her gaze met his, he leaned closer, drawn as if by an invisible magnet to her lips. "The only thing that's happened is that I think I'm starting to fall—"

A loud alert blared from her phone. "Starting to what?" Her voice came out strangled, but she never broke eye contact.

"Don't you want to know what that was?"

"Just a weather alert." She shrugged. "How bad can it be this time of year?"

The distance between them faded away and he slid a hand into her hair as his lips at last brushed hers. Warm and waiting. So sweet, so soft.

He eased her onto the bed, sliding his hand up

beneath her blouse. Her warm breast filled his palm.

She gasped, her eyes meeting his for a split second before she nodded and tugged her blouse up over her head. The sight of the pink lace, her rosy areola and swollen nipple showing through was nearly his undoing. Oh, yes, he'd been wanting this moment for a long time.

He sat up, yanked his sweater over his head and made it a point to toss it over the snow globe. She slid her hands eagerly over his chest. He uttered a silent prayer of thanks for all the time he spent working out.

"So this is what you were hiding under that ugly Christmas sweater." She reached behind her to unclasp her bra.

"And this is what you were hiding under those bulky sweatshirts." He grinned as his lips found their way back to hers, his hands taking the time to leisurely explore her breasts while their mouths got to know one another.

He bent his head, working his way down her neck, to her chest, and at last, to her breasts. The rosy peaks against her pale skin reminded him of berries and cream and he couldn't wait to taste…

A shudder moved through her as his tongue flicked across her nipple. "Jake, it's been a really long time for me…I don't want you to think…"

Why did women always want to talk at such a moment? He pulled the nipple between his lips, rewarded by her moan of pleasure. Her fingers tangled into his hair. "I mean for all we know you could be married, or…"

"Shh…Luce," he whispered against her soft skin. "We'll talk more about it later, I promise."

She nodded. "I know. I want you to know that I don't expect anything. Whatever happens…I just need you now. Chocolate chip cookies and all." She reached for his jeans, tugging at the button. How could he deny a request like that? Yes, he should explain things, put her mind at ease…tell her she was involved with someone who wasn't totally human. But there would be time for that later.

As if they had mutually decided to do so at the same time, they both rose and quickly removed the rest of their clothes.

They came together on the bed in a tangle of arms and legs, kissing and touching, him fumbling for the protection he'd left on the nightstand. At last he slid into her warm, welcoming body. She cried out and wrapped her legs high about his waist, her heels holding him to her as he rocked against her. Her insides quivered and squeezed around him, and he pulled back, thrusting deeper until he tumbled over the edge right after her.

For long moments the sound of their own heavy breathing was all he could hear. The feel of her legs, cool and silky, tangled with his. He tugged her against him, drowsy, sated.

And then it began.

A series of incoming message chimes from her phone. Not just one. Dozens.

With a groan, he untangled himself from her to allow her to reach to the floor for her phone.

"I'm beginning to think I'm sorry I ever replaced my phone…" She picked up the intrusive device. "Let me just turn it off—oh my God."

"What is it?"

"That weather alert was for a blizzard. I guess it just came in out of nowhere and they're warning people to seek shelter immediately." She brushed her thumb over the screen. "The rest of the messages are from the other merchants. They are closing early, want to know if I am home and okay, if I need anything. Barbara is worried because I didn't answer her last text. Let me just…" She began to tap the virtual keyboard.

A strong gust of wind rattled the window. Jake rose, not bothering to cover himself, and pulled the cord to open the curtains. A solid wall of white was all that was visible through the blowing snow.

Lucy's mouth dropped open. She rose so abruptly her phone tumbled to the floor. "What is that?"

He ran a hand down his face. "I'm guessing that is what happens when you piss off a snow princess."

Chapter Eleven

Lucy frowned. She had no idea what Jake meant by that, but it was the least of her concerns.

He switched on the TV where a local reporter reported live from outside the news station. Wind whipped the woman's hair across her face, and she held onto her hat with one hand while trying to maintain her cheery persona.

Lucy's phone blared another alert and she glanced at the screen. *Shelter in place. No unnecessary travel.* "I've got to go." She grabbed her clothes off the floor and hurriedly shrugged into them. No hat, no gloves. Her only scarf was silky and decorative, not really suited for the walk home in a snowstorm. For a moment, she wondered if leaving was the best idea.

"It is snowmageddon out here, guys, with near zero visibility," chirped the reporter over the howling wind. "The sheriff's department is closing the roads as we speak, and thruway authorities have shut down all exits between…"

Jake switched off the TV and reached for his clothes. "Luce, are you crazy? You can't go out there."

"I have to get home. My phone battery is nearly dead, and I left the *Be Right Back* sign on the door of the store. It's locked, but…"

He placed his hands on her shoulders. The warmth of his skin seeped through her sweater and the comforting, familiar cookie aroma swirled around her. She stared into his deep blue eyes, willing herself not to remember what they had just done.

Spending the night here with him would only lead to her wanting much more, and she still didn't know anything about him. Other than his lips were soft and warm, and he tasted as good as he smelled and making love with him was the most wonderful thing she'd ever experienced…

"I don't think anyone will come by the store tonight. Let's just wait and see what happens. Maybe the whole thing will blow over as fast as it began." His gaze held hers. "In fact, I really wish the storm would stop."

She frowned at the way he enunciated those last words. Something strange was going on, but then she'd had that feeling since he had appeared in the middle of Main Street the other day.

From over his shoulder the sight outside the window caught her attention. "Jake—look, the snow has stopped!"

He whirled to look, and a relived sigh rushed out of him. "It worked."

"Y—you did that." A strange trembling sensation began in her stomach, traveling to her arms, then down her legs until they nearly buckled. She sank onto the edge of the bed, trying desperately to draw a deep breath. "You made it stop snowing."

"What? Come on, just a freak coincidence."

It was all so clear now. "The ornaments you found in my basement. You made that happen, too. And the Christmas trees…"

"Luce, you're talking crazy."

"Who are you? And *don't* give me the amnesia story

because you don't seem to be in any hurry to find out, which tells me—"

He folded his arms and regarded her with those piercing blue eyes. "Tells you what?"

She jumped to her feet. "That I need to go. It's not snowing anymore; I need to get home before anything else weird happens. For all I know there's a Christmas tree growing through the ceiling into my living room by now…" She hurried to the door, eager for the feel of cool air on her face, praying it would clear her head. How was it possible that just moments ago they were joined together, and everything was pure bliss?

Jake wiped a hand down his face. "Fine, I'll explain. Just come back in and sit down."

"No, I think I'm good right where I am." She held onto the doorknob, not sure why, but at the moment it felt like the only link between her and a complete mental breakdown.

"You're right, to a certain point. It's all been me, or at least because of me." He paced to one side of the room.

She tightened her hand on the knob, squeezing so hard it hurt. "I don't understand."

"I'm not from around here, Luce. I know you've guessed that already."

A thousand questions ran through her head, but she didn't vocalize them. He took the hint and paced to the other side of the room.

"I'm from north of here."

"Canada," she rasped, recalling the conversation.

"Farther north."

Oh, she didn't like where this was heading. This was the part where Jake would take a detour into Crazy Town. She knew he was too good to be true, all the cute ones were… "How much farther north?"

"A lot."

She swallowed, praying he would say something normal. "A—Alaska?"

He shoved a hand through his hair. "It's not so different from here really. We live Christmas every day up there, too. You might say it's our business."

A bubble of laughter came out before she could stop it. "Let me guess, and you make toys that get delivered to children around the world on December—" the solemn expression on his face stopped her cold. "Oh dear God." Yep, he was nuts.

As if the floodgates had opened, he started talking. Being half elf and half human, Nick Claus being his Godfather. His mother wanting him to be more responsible and sending him to the human world. Having to decide where he wanted to live.

She listened, half in horror, half in fascination until he stopped talking. "So…what are you saying?"

"I'm saying I can fix this. All of it." He pulled a pocket watch from his jeans and flipped it open. "Except I'm almost out of magic, stopping that snowstorm took a lot. But I can do it—I can get Nick to come back, spread a little magic around the town like he used to—and I can ask around, see if some of the other elves can—"

Elves. That was it. She was done listening. She closed the hotel room door as soundlessly as possible and walked out of the room and down the hall. Only when she reached the doors to the outside and the cool air hit her face did she break into a run.

****

The snick of the door latch stopped Jake in mid-sentence. When he turned around, Lucy had gone.

And little wonder with him ranting like an escapee from the loony bin. He grabbed his jacket, intent on going after her. He'd have to prove it to her somehow, make her understand that he wasn't crazy. But how? His pocket watch was clearly in the red, as he'd tried to show her. Stopping that storm had taken more of his magic than he'd expected. He could kick himself for that, he should have just let things be, convinced her to spend the night and then explained things, or better yet just showed her.

The snow globe. That would do it. He grabbed it from the nightstand, tucked it into his duffel bag and headed for the door.

A figure clad in body hugging red fleece appeared, blocking his path. "Hi Jakey."

"Flora—"

"Fauna," she corrected. "Flora is too upset to ever talk to you again."

"Why, because I'm interested in someone else?"

"Because you were mean to her." She pushed away from the door and sauntered across the room. "And because you interfered with her snowstorm."

"Look, I'd love to stay and reminisce, but I'm kind of in a hurry."

She took a seat on the end of the bed and studied her shiny red fingernails. She blinked and an emery board appeared in one hand. "She tried to warn you, Jake. Really, do you think an elf can halt a storm created by one of Jack Frost's daughters?"

"Well, I just did."

"More like paused it." She nodded toward the window. "I brought in some reinforcements."

As she spoke a loud clap of thunder rumbled across

the sky. Snow began to blow past the window again.

"Daddy wasn't happy to hear you made Flora cry. And Gale decided to send a nice wind storm your way. You know how she likes those."

"Why would she do that?"

One slim shoulder lifted in a shrug. "She was very motivated once I told her you'd called her fat."

"What?" He nearly dropped his duffel bag. "I never did."

"Oopsie." She giggled.

A rumbling at the window drew his attention. The trees in the park across the street began to bend as a ferocious wind whipped through.

Fauna held up a finger. "Oh there she is now." She glanced at the window, then gave a little smile. "Now you know why Mummy and Daddy named her Gale Force Wind."

The sound of ice pellets hitting the window came next and Fauna smiled as she gently sawed at one of her nails. "And that would be Daddy." She rubbed her arms and gave a little shiver. "Not a nice night to be out there is it?"

Lucy.

He hurried to the door, her laughter echoing in his ears as he made his way down the hallway.

As he reached the doors to exit the building, a tell-tale snap came from outside followed by a boom that shook the ground.

And then the lodge went dark.

Chapter Twelve

A shower of green sparks lit the sky in the distance. Lucy had seen enough ice and windstorms to recognize the crack and boom of falling branches and the lights from arcing power lines.

Which brought little comfort, buffeted as she was by gusty winds, snow and ice. And now cast into darkness without even a streetlight to help her see.

Should she turn around and head back to the lodge? Or keep moving forward—at least she *hoped* it was forward.

She tugged the edges of her jacket closer, tucked the scarf over her nose and mouth and pushed onward. The light jacket and loafers—*loafer* since one foot was still wrapped in a slipper sock—were no help against the rapidly falling snow and chill, so she tried to focus on how good it would feel once she got home. A long bubble bath. Some hot cocoa. Maybe a whole pot of hot cocoa. The electric blanket on her bed…well, once the power was back on, anyway.

The streets were deserted and the whiteouts at the corner intersection made it impossible to tell when she'd fully crossed the street. She hit the curb with the toe of her shoe and stumbled forward, reaching both hands out to catch her fall.

Ice and cold filled her palms and she struggled to her feet. Great. Now she was wet from the knees down. She reached out a hand to check if there was a building nearby and felt the cold window front of one of the stores. She continued moving down Main Street, feeling her way along until she came to a doorway. She huddled there for a second or two, away from the breathtaking wind.

If she survived this, she would never complain about a hot summer day again.

"Lucy!" Jake called over the howling wind as he hurried through the streets. The pocket watch felt warm against his thigh. He'd already wished for warmer outerwear. He wasn't sure how much magic he had left.

How the hell did Nick travel through this stuff? Sure, not every Christmas Eve brought snowstorms, but he usually encountered bad weather at some point during his travels; Jake had heard enough of the stories.

Wind whipped at his nose and cheeks, the snow hitting his face like fine grit sandpaper. His fingertips, even in the thick gloves, already felt cold.

Lucy was out here in just a light jacket. The thought sent an urgency to his footsteps as he hurried across the parking lot. At least he was pretty sure it was the parking lot.

What the hell were Flora and Fauna thinking anyway, conjuring up a sudden storm like this? *Snow princesses, my ass*. More like spoiled little girls. And maybe that's why he'd never seen them as anything more than playmates. Vain and shallow, only interested in clothes, makeup, or themselves.

Nothing like Lucy.

Why had he gone and told her the truth now? What was he thinking? More like what had he been thinking *with*. He'd wanted her to spend the night, wanted to assure her he had no other attachments, hoping that would convince her to stay. But instead he came across like a lunatic, the very thing he'd wanted to avoid.

He came to the park and decided to cross that rather than take his chances with the roads. With the power out and people trying to get home from work, it was a confusing mess. He heard more than one screech of tires followed by banging metal.

He just hoped Lucy had the sense to cut across the park, too.

He dodged a falling branch being carried on the wind and sidestepped another on the ground. He felt a connection to Lucy, a true connection he'd never noticed with any other woman. And it wasn't just sex.

There was something about her that pulled at him.

Up ahead he could barely make out a shape in the white haze but as he grew closer, he recognized the gazebo. For a moment, the memory of sitting there with her, surrounded by the soft glow of twinkle lights came over him. It was her special place; she'd told him that much.

Please let her be here. "Luce!" he called over the wind. "Luce, are you here?"

No answer.

Damn, she must have tried to get back to the shop. He turned, hoping his sense of direction wasn't leading him astray and headed that way.

Snowmobile goggles, that's what he needed to help him see through this stuff. He uttered a wish for them, pausing to wait for them to appear.

Nothing.

He wished again, slower and more insistent this time.

Nothing.

The gloves were too thick for him to reach into his pocket, but he patted it, wanting to make sure the watch was still in place. Yep, still there. But cold. No warmth from trying to grant a wish.

Shit, was he out of magic?

A pang of panic shot through him at the thought. How was he going to find her on his own?

He shook his head. What was he thinking? This weather was a piece of cake for the North Pole, nothing he couldn't handle.

He put his head down and trudged into the wind.

****

She'd walked past this building already, hadn't she? Was she going in circles? Her nose felt like an icicle and her feet and hands were numb. The pitch-dark street and wind-whipped snow made it hard to tell if she was on Main Street, Second Street—or the middle of nowhere.

How could she possibly be this lost in her own hometown?

She rubbed her arms, failing to find any warmth from the friction. Well, this was a fine mess. She stumbled against a step. And decided to sit. It was impossible to know whose store it was. Well, she would just wait right here for the owner to show up. For some reason that made the most sense.

She huddled into a ball and waited. It was nice here. Sheltered from the worst of the wind gusts. And warm. She felt better now, thank goodness. She rested her head against the cold stone wall and closed her eyes.

Why did he have to be crazy? There were worse things in the world than loving someone who thought they were an elf. Maybe that was the amnesia talking, maybe when she shoved him to the ground and he hit his head, he decided he was an elf. But that didn't explain the smell of chocolate chip cookies that came from him, or the warm fuzzy memories they evoked when he touched her.

She could tolerate a little crazy in her life, right? So why had she left, if she had just stayed there they'd be cuddled under the covers right now, making love and talking about the North Pole…

"Luce!"

The sound of Jake's voice brought a smile to her insides. Oh, he had such a sexy voice. She could almost smell the chocolate chip cookies…

"Can we leave some carrots for the reindeer, Grandma?"

"I have it on very good authority that those reindeer prefer jellybeans," boomed Grandpa's jolly voice. "Jellybeans and…potato chips." His bushy eyebrows wiggled up and down.

She giggled and reached for another cookie.

"You'll spoil your dinner, Lucy," Grandma scolded. "And you need to leave some of those cookies for Santa. Young lady, did you hear me?"

"Luce! Can you hear me?"

She stirred. The smell of warm chocolate chip cookies filled her nostrils now and she pulled it in deep, savoring it. Something touched her skin, but she was so cold she almost couldn't feel it.

"Thank God. Here," the sound of a zipper being undone met her ears and she was lifted off the ground and felt… warmth. Her body reacted violently, and she began to shiver.

"You're okay," Jake's voice soothed. "You'll be

okay."

It seemed they were moving, though the pace was slow. The sound of his breathing met her ear, but she focused on the comfort of the cookie aroma.

"Here we are. Let's get you inside." She was set down on something cold, and moaned a protest at the loss of his warmth. The loud sound of glass shattering reached her ears. She was lifted again, and warmth surrounded her.

"I'll get something to put over that door in a few minutes. First things first." He set her on something soft. And it wasn't cold. She flopped down.

"No, no, no. Stay with me. "You're going to have to trust me now, Luce. I need to undress you."

For some reason those words struck her as funny, and a giggle bubbled up from deep inside. "I've already been naked with you, Jake."

"We can talk about that later. Come on, lift your arms…"

The cold wet fabric brushed against her face as her shirt was pulled over her head.

"Aw geez, you and that pink lace, you really know how to torment a guy. Okay that's wet so it's coming off too, I promise not to look…much."

Her bra was removed and then the warm jacket he'd draped over her was wrapped around her again.

"Now the jeans—Are there pink lace panties to match that bra? I should have looked earlier but we were in such a hurry. If there are, I swear I'll kick myself…" He talked as he undressed her. Her jeans were wet and heavy and the cold material took a lot of wriggling to come down her hips. There was a soft thwack as they hit the floor in a wet heap.

"Let me get a blanket first." He wrapped the blanket from the couch around her waist and then reached underneath.

The touch of his fingers brushing her thighs brought on a case of the tickles as he pulled the wet panties down and off.

"There. Who says I can't be a gentleman?"

She rested her head back on the sofa. A violent shivering began to take hold.

"I'm just going to get the key out of your pants and go upstairs to get more blankets, Luce. Then I'm going to put some cardboard over that door."

She barely paid attention as the need for sleep came over her. She stirred only a little when heavy blankets were tucked around her and something warm was tugged onto her feet. She moaned a protest when the jacket was pulled out from around her and cool air met her bare skin, but soon something soft was hauled over her head and her arms were threaded into sleeves.

"Let me pull the hood over your hair, it will warm you faster," he murmured near her ear. The soft tickle of his words touched her ear, and she grinned again. "Jake, why d'you have to be so damn sexy." She moaned. "And crazy."

"Well, you can't have everything," he said.

"Maybe," she sighed. "But I was kind of falling for you…"

"Me too, Luce. Me too."

****

Jake kept a close eye on Lucy as he worked to repair the door. He should have just looked for the key in her pocket instead of smashing the glass on the door, but he hadn't thought of that in the moment. He'd just wanted to get her inside.

But as she slept, the color gradually returned to her cheeks.

When he'd finished with the door, he dragged a chair out from behind the cash register and placed it near her. He pulled the pocket watch out and studied it. Red. Totally red. Did that mean he could no longer get home?

Well, it didn't matter. Saving Lucy was worth it. Now he had just one more thing to do and then he'd be out of her hair for good. But he'd let her sleep first.

He must have dozed off in the chair because sudden movement startled him. He opened his eyes and locked gazes with her. She sat up on the couch, looking warily around. She'd pulled some of the blankets off, that was a good sign.

"Hi," he said, feeling like he could melt right into those gingerbread brown eyes of hers.

She reached up to tug the hood from her head and looked at the sweatshirt he'd put on her in disbelief. "I don't remember wearing this. Or lying here. How…"

He explained all of it, at least from the time she left the hotel. He didn't want to re-hash the argument they'd had or what he'd shared with her about himself.

A half smile turned up the corner of her mouth. "So…did you use your elf magic to find me?"

"No." He swallowed past a sudden lump of emotion. "I don't possess any of my own magic and what I had… well, I used it all on something else."

"I see." She studied his face. "Jake, I'm sorry for what I said. You can imagine how it sounds to me. I mean something was off about you, that was clear from the start but…"

"I know." He reached for the duffel bag he'd left

near the sofa, waiting for this moment. "Look, I just want to show you something, and then I'll be on my way, you won't have to see me again."

Panic flickered briefly in her eyes but when he held the snow globe out to her, she took it.

"Just stare into it for a moment and tell me what you see." She frowned but did as he asked. "It's glowing. Sort of a bluish white color. Am I supposed to see something?"

"Yes, just keep watching." He wasn't sure how long it would take for her to forget that she knew him, but from what he'd heard it didn't take long.

"I don't think I understand—"

He reached for the button on the bottom of the snow globe, the one that would create the flash to erase her memories of him.

"Just keep watching, it's worth the wait, you'll see."

"Jake, stop!"

Lucy let out a shriek as Merry's face appeared in the globe. She tossed the snow globe aside and jumped to her feet. "Is that supposed to be funny?"

"No—she's not supposed to be in there." But even as he said it, a waft of cinnamon and vanilla filled the room and his mother appeared before them.

Lucy took a step backward, eyes wide as saucers. "How'd you do that? You came out of…." She pointed to the glowing orb on the floor. "That!"

"Hi, honey," Merry said in her sweetest voice. "I'm sorry I startled you. But I had to stop him."

Jake had a hard time pulling his gaze from the sight of Lucy's long pale legs. His sweatshirt only came to her thighs. How had he not noticed her great legs earlier when they made love?

Lucy caught him looking and glanced down. "This is not my sweatshirt. What the hell is the NPA?" She held the front of it out and tried to read the red and green logo.

"North Pole Academy, where Dash went to elf school," Merry explained. "Hon, you look like you've seen a ghost, why don't you sit down and let me explain."

"I'm good." Lucy backed up to the fireplace. "Wh—who is Dash?"

"Long story," Jake murmured.

"How about some tea?" Merry asked. She blinked and a steaming cup appeared in her hands.

Lucy shook her head. "I'm pretty sure I'm hallucinating, so no thanks."

"Ma, you can't just barge in here and—"

"This is your *mother*?" Lucy's eyes went wide. "Wait a minute. I've seen you somewhere before. And that smell—it's been everywhere lately."

Jake wiped a hand down his face. "Lucy, meet Merry Mistletoe, my mother. She's the one behind the appearance of the Christmas trees."

Chapter Thirteen

Lucy couldn't help starting at the woman before her. Tiny, dressed in a red and green outfit and slippers with turned up toes and jingle bells. Curly russet hair and pointed ears stuck out from beneath her red and green hat. She looked exactly like what she'd imagined an elf from the North Pole would look like.

An elf! She put a hand to her forehead. Was she dreaming or dead? She must be dreaming; Jake had put all of this in her head.

Merry looked out the window at the swirling wall of white. "Dash, what is going on here? Why are they having such terrible weather? I only asked Jack to send a little snow. I don't remember seeing anything like this when we were here before."

"H—here?" Lucy asked. "You were here?" Wait, hadn't Jake said something about that—elves coming to help out with the parade?

Jake glanced at his mother and pulled a face. "The Frost twins."

"This?" Merry gestured toward the window. "Those two girls did all this?"

"Gale helped and I guess Jack, too."

Frost twins? Jack? Oh dear God. Lucy's knees began to wobble. In the blink of an eye a comfortable chair appeared behind her and a hot cup of tea in her hands.

"I'll save the I told you so's for now, Dash, but let me fix this mess…"

Lucy watched, fascinated, as the tiny woman waved her arms. She leaned forward, and stared out the window as the wind and snow came to an abrupt halt.

"I could put the tree limbs back and restore the power, but that would be a lot harder for people to accept. And we can't go around erasing everyone's memories."

Alarm jolted Lucy. "Erasing *whose* memory?"

"Oh that," Merry laughed and the sound reminded Lucy of tinkling bells. "That's what I wanted to talk to Dash about."

"Is that what that's for?" she asked, pointing to the snow globe on the floor between them. "You were going to…"

Jake sighed. "I thought you'd be better off not remembering you ever met me."

A hot ball of anger shot up her spine. She set the cup aside and rose from the chair. "You can't decide something like that without asking me. Maybe I want to remember you, did you ever think of that?"

Merry perched on the arm of the sofa and studied them both. "This is what I wanted to stop you from doing Da—Jake." She shook her head. "I don't know why an elf name isn't good enough for you, son." She sighed. "Don't make the mistake I did. I've regretted it my entire life."

"What mistake?" Lucy wished she was still standing against the fireplace, she wanted something solid to lean against.

Merry studied her for a moment, as though deciding what to say. "When I was young I fell in love. With a human. I told him the truth about who I was. He couldn't

246

handle it." She shook her head and when her bright green eyes met Lucy's, they were tormented. "Rather than try to work it out—or fight for him, I took the easy way out and erased his memory. I found out afterward I was pregnant with Dash—Jake." She swiped at a tear. "It is still the biggest regret of my life. Not only did I deny myself the man I loved, but I also denied Jake his father."

A lump of emotion lodged in Lucy's throat. She gazed at Jake, trying to imagine what it would be like to never see him again, never know he existed. She'd rather have the pain of having loved him and lost him than to go through life never knowing him.

"And his father… you never saw him again?"

Merry sniffled and blinked a cup of tea into her hand. "Oh, I've seen him. Not to speak to him, but in a crowd once or twice years ago. He's happily married now with no memory of me."

"In a crowd?" Jake pushed away from his stance near the sofa. "Wait a second. Is that why we were here for the parade?" He smacked a palm to his forehead. "Is this where you came when you visited the real world? That's why you sent me here, you were remembering him when you zapped me."

Merry shrugged. "I couldn't help myself."

"Wait—visited the real world? Zapped you?" Lucy couldn't keep up. "I'm really confused here, guys."

The bells on the door jingled as it was pulled open.

"Luce?" Rick's voice came from around the corner. "I saw the cardboard on the door and was worried something—" He took in the sight of her clad only in a sweatshirt, of Jake looking rather sheepish.

And then his blue gaze swung to the woman in the elf outfit. "Merry Mistletoe."

****

From the warm glow of lights in the coffee shop, the one place in town that had power—thanks to a little elf magic—Lucy sat with Jake, studying the couple at the table nearby. Their heads were together, their voices low and hushed.

"Of all people to be my father," Jake said with a shake of his head. "That guy hates me."

"I wonder why I never noticed before that you have his eyes," Lucy mused. "But don't you think it's romantic? He recognized her. It's like his mind forgot her but his heart never did."

From what they'd been able to piece together, Rick and Merry had met during her time in Christmasville, they'd worked together at the Christmas Tree Farm. But when the holiday season ended and it came time for Merry to leave, she'd confessed the truth to Rick. And much like Lucy, he hadn't taken it well. Which led to a memory erasing via snow globe.

Now Rick was understandably confused but the details Merry shared and the fact that he had associated her name with the aromas of vanilla and cinnamon, that he'd spent a lifetime pining for something he couldn't remember made sense. And when he'd confessed he often dreamed of Merry without knowing who she was or why, Lucy's heart nearly broke in two.

Jake's hand over hers brought her out of her thoughts. "I don't want that to be us."

"Me either." She studied him, finally able to see him through different eyes. He wasn't crazy and he didn't have amnesia. But was it okay to let herself feel everything she was feeling? "Jake, where do we go from here? My life is up in the air right now and you have a

248

job to get home to."

He squeezed her hand. "Come with me, Luce. Leave the fake Christmas world behind and come live with me in the real one."

She looked around her. Could she really do it? Leave her old life behind and begin a new one with him? For some reason, the choice that seemed so painful hours ago, the feeling her life was changing too fast, didn't feel so scary anymore. As long as she was with him she didn't care where they were.

He scooted his chair closer and wrapped his other hand over hers. "If you hate it there, we'll come back."

A heaviness settled over her. "To what? A superstore and a bookstore chain?" She glanced up as Merry and Rick rose and moved across the room to study the pictures along the wall.

Jake looked over his shoulder to follow her gaze. "Well, I think you may have someone on your side who can help revitalize the town." He stroked Lucy's hand with his thumb. "Obviously, this place means a lot to her, or she wouldn't have sent me here."

Lucy leaned closer to press her lips to his. "Well, I'm glad she did."

The smell of chocolate chip cookies filled her nostrils and warmth and happy memories flooded her as his lips brushed hers.

"Okay you two, enough of that." She looked up to see Rick approaching with Merry at his side, holding his hand. He glanced at Jake a bit sheepishly. "I guess I'll have to stop asking why you're still here. We have a lot of catching up to do. And a lot of explaining. I was just on my way to pick up Madison."

"That's right, I have a little sister," Jake said with a

laugh. "I'm not an only child anymore."

As Rick and Merry turned to head out into the night, Jake rose and tugged Lucy to her feet. "Care to come back to my place?"

Heat filled her insides at the thought of being alone with him again. "Mine's closer."

She slipped her hand into his and they left the coffee shop, making sure to lock up on their way out. The street was quiet, but trucks from the power company were parked down the street, yellow lights flashing as they got to work.

They paused at the corner. "Is this where you pushed me into oncoming traffic?" Jake asked.

"Right in the middle of this intersection," she said as the crossed the street. She glanced back, realizing that as they passed the Christmas trees Merry had placed about town, one by one, the lights were going on despite the power still being out.

"Jake…are you sure you don't possess any Christmas magic of your own?"

He gave her hand a tight squeeze. "Nope. I had a fifty-fifty shot; I was either going to get elf genes or human ones. But I suppose if I ever have kids some day they could inherit the elf magic. Why?"

As they passed another tree, the lights suddenly switched on. "Um…no reason."

Lucy put a hand to her abdomen in wonder. Could it be?

Maybe there was more to those Chocolate Chip Christmas wishes than she'd realized.

Epilogue

One Year Later
Thanksgiving Day

Lucy swayed back and forth, rocking little Dash in his baby sling even though he slept soundly through the noise of the excited crowd. She bent to place a kiss to his head and tug his hat down a bit more snugly over his pointed ears.

It was the perfect day for a parade and the entire town had turned out to see it along with hundreds of tourists. A movement at her side caught her eye and she turned to see Barbara rushing toward her, arms open for a hug.

"Oooh, let me get my hands on that precious baby."

Lucy lifted him from the carrier that kept him snug to her chest and handed him over. He barely stirred.

Her friend lifted him almost reverently and placed a kiss to his cheek. "Lord, he even smells new." She placed him to her shoulder, patting his back with the familiarity of someone who'd held dozens of babies.

By now Tim and Brad had also spotted her and hurried over to visit.

As the floats began to move down the street, they cheered and waved. First up came a float advertising the Reindeer Lodge, with Mr. and Mrs. Kim waving to the crowd and tossing out discount vouchers.

Next was Laura, the Christmasville town historian, reading to a group of children in a Night Before Christmas themed float.

After catching up on each other's lives over the past several months, talk turned to the changes in their little town.

"How is Frieda?" Lucy asked.

Barbara rolled her eyes. "Well, she's still pretty upset about the money she missed out on when that deal fell through."

"We all were," Tim chimed in. "We were already looking at condos in Florida when the developer pulled out."

"And there was no explanation given?"

"They just said they'd found a better location." Brad waved a hand through the air. "Whatever. I can tolerate a few more New York winters if business stays like this."

"So things have been good?" Lucy asked, even as guilt gnawed at her over the abrupt changes to everyone's plans. Just as Jake had suspected, Merry had a soft spot for Christmasville. Though she didn't know why the developers had pulled their offers abruptly just before Christmas last year, she suspected a little elfin magic had been at work.

"Better than good," Barbara said. "Ever since that Christmas tree miracle last year, tourists have been coming back like crazy. We've all been able to afford to redecorate our shops and hire part time help. It's like the old days, only better."

"Part time help means we can take a vacation when we need to," Brad added with a nod. "So maybe we can't buy that Florida condo yet, but we spend a lot of time down there anyway."

"And everyone else is okay, too?" Lucy asked.

"Okay? Girl, your mother-in-law is a force of nature. She and Rick have singlehandedly transformed this town." Barbara gestured toward a float that featured trees from the Mistletoe Christmas Tree Farm, with Rick, Merry and Madison waving and tossing out candy canes.

Lucy smiled as warmth bathed her insides. Of all the changes this past year, perhaps the most surprising was Merry's decision to retire from her position as head elf to join Rick and Madison permanently in Christmasville.

Rick had sold the coffee shop to a younger couple who had a lot more energy to run it. And Rick and Merry had bought and reopened the tree farm where they first met. Merry had recently been elected mayor running on a platform to modernize the town and return it to its roots as a year-round Christmas destination.

"So Pam and Sarita are still supplying the baked good for the coffee shop?" she asked.

Brad nodded. "And they opened a yoga studio just a block or so over; it's been a huge hit. Here they are now."

He pointed toward a float with the two ladies dressed in yoga gear waving to the crowd while others on the float held various yoga poses.

"And my grandparents' store?" Lucy swallowed past a lump of emotion.

"Oh, baby, it's in good hands. Frieda and her husband are having the time of their lives with it. They were both so tired of corporate life and this gives them more time with the kids." Barbara's dark eyes welled with emotion. "You did your best, honey. Your grandparents would want you to live *your* life, not theirs."

It warmed her to know a new generation was staking

a claim in the town, but she still felt such a connection to it. Christmasville would always be home.

But Barbara was right; Lucy was finally living her own life. Jake had moved into Merry's role as head elf, and she loved their home at the North Pole. During off season they traveled. Even though she had been pregnant through most of their travels so far she had managed to see more of the world than she'd ever imagined in just a few short months.

The aroma of chocolate chip cookies announced Jake's arrival moments before he came into sight. He'd been helping with some of the floats for the parade. One in particular.

"Is he all set?" Lucy asked as her husband slipped his arm about her waist.

"He's great, says it's like riding a bike. He still remembers how." He winked at her. "It's not like he hasn't been doing this for a couple hundred years."

At last the float everyone had been waiting to see rounded the corner. Santa—the real Santa, though a year ago she'd barely believed in his existence, waved from his seat on the float. A cheer went through the crowd.

As the float moved past, an incredible feeling of joy and happiness filled the air.

Lucy looked around to see if it was just her, but it wasn't. Kids were starry eyed, parents smiled from ear to ear and even little Dash lifted his head from Barbara's shoulder for a moment, as if he, too, felt it.

Christmas magic was in the air once more in Christmasville.

9 781509 244836